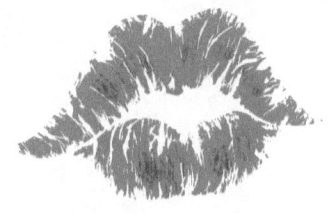

EVERNIGHT PUBLISHING ®

www.evernightpublishing.com

SAM CRESCENT

Copyright© 2021

Sam Crescent

Editor: Karyn White

Cover Art: Sour Cherry Designs

Jacket Design: Jay Aheer

ISBN: 978-0-3695-0303-9

ALL RIGHTS RESERVED

DEATH'S DIRTY DEMANDS

DEATH'S DIRTY DEMANDS

Chaos Bleeds, 5

Sam Crescent

Copyright © 2014

Chapter One

"What the fuck do you think you're doing?" Devil asked, glaring at Lexie. Death sat at the bar watching his president lose his shit.

"I'm decorating the clubhouse. We're having Christmas here. I don't care what you say, Devil. We're all alive after the crap that went down with Gonzalez. So we're not going to get a visit from Tiny and his crew, but we're going to celebrate this holiday season like the club we are."

"I don't give a shit about Christmas. I want to know why my woman, heavily pregnant, is standing on a fucking stool hanging decorations when there are men on their asses, and prospects to do the fucking work." Devil glared around the room at the men who were watching. Dick, Butler, Snake, Spider, and Dime all got to their feet. Death joined in as well, grabbing the balloons he spotted in the corner. Sitting at the bar, he began to blow each of them up, tie the end, before flicking it into the room.

"This is what you call fucking helping?" Devil asked, taking a seat beside him. "Woman's going to give me a fucking heart attack. She shouldn't be doing shit like that being all pregnant."

"You're the one who knocked her up. It's your responsibility." Death handed Devil a balloon and laughed at the disgust on Devil's face.

"Fucking woman is going to be the death of me. Judi's not much better."

Death glanced over to see Ripper and Judi cuddled together in the corner. They were sat on the floor with Judi holding up a pregnancy book. Ripper had his hands on his woman's stomach. They were a beautiful sight, and something hit Death in the chest. Ever since they'd settled in Piston County the guys had started to settle down, finding women who were worth more than a quick fuck.

"Hey, Devil. Can I get you anything?"

He tensed as he heard the small voice that had come to plague his thoughts on a daily basis.

"Fuck, I can't drink yet. Get me a coffee, honey." Devil didn't look behind him at the redhead.

Out of the corner of Death's eye, he saw her, Brianna Wentworth. She'd been one of the women they'd gotten out of the titty bar before they burnt it to the ground. There were only a handful of women who'd stayed around the club, becoming club whores for the men who wanted them. Brianna, the red-haired siren with her shocking green eyes, she'd stayed to work at the club. She'd become like a cleaner, cook, barmaid, and general errands girl. Not one man had fucked her as far as Death knew. They'd left her alone. He tried to stay away from her. She was too damn young for a man like him. He was in his late thirties, almost forty. She had just turned twenty. A couple of days ago he'd heard one of his club brothers ask her how old she was. At least she wasn't younger. Gonzalez hadn't cared about the women he sold or their age.

Thinking about the man they'd put into the ground filled Death with hatred. Gonzalez had entered their lives and fucked with them, before being killed in Fort Wills. The Chaos Bleeds no longer had a working relationship with The Skulls. He knew Lexie and the kids visited with Eva, but that was it.

Simon, Devil's son, walked up to the bar to where Death was sitting.

He watched him climb onto a stool, putting the piece of paper that was now rumpled, onto the surface. Death chuckled as Simon started to pull out all of his crayons.

"What ya doing, son?" Devil asked.

"I'm writing a card." Simon didn't look up from the paper. "Dad, how do you spell Tabitha?"

Death watched as Devil tensed in his seat.

"Why?"

"I'm writing a card to Tabitha. She won't be coming for Christmas, and I want her to remember me."

"She's a little girl."

"So, she's my friend."

Lexie walked up, stroking Simon's head. "T ... A ... B..."

Death tuned out, reaching for his drink only to find the soda empty.

"Would you like me to get you another?" Brianna asked. She rested her palm on the edge of the counter. Her gaze was on him with her amazing eyes. Fuck, he loved her eyes. They held a wealth of emotion and were so fucking expressive. Even now, he saw she was nervous, yet intrigued by the club. Over the past couple of months he'd seen when she was excited, scared, aroused, all of it there for him to see. It was like her eyes held a glimpse to her soul. They told him what he needed to hear. Her body always betrayed her as well.

Being part of Chaos Bleeds when they used to move around from place to place, never staying for long, he'd become adept at reading people. He didn't have much choice but to trust his instincts. The majority of the time his instincts were spot on.

"Yeah, I'll have another soda."

She nodded, turning away to bend over. Snake chose that time to come to the bar.

"Fuck me," Snake said.

Death saw what he was looking at. Landing a blow to his friend's stomach, he shook his head in warning.

"You tapping that?" Snake asked.

Death shook his head.

"Here you are," Brianna said, smiling at both men. She was completely clueless to what was happening between him and Snake. "Can I get you anything?"

"Snake's good. He can serve himself," Death said.

She nodded and moved away from the bar out of earshot.

"You're not tapping that and you're not letting anyone else tap it?" Snake asked.

"She's too young." Most of the guys had steered clear of the women they'd saved from Gonzalez's clutches. Brianna was one of those women, but there would come a time when she'd need to make a choice. The men wouldn't keep their hands off forever.

"She was taken by Gonzalez, Death. I'm sure she knows what happens between the birds and the bees."

"What's the birds and the bees?" Simon asked.

Devil shot them both a glare. "It's nothing, son. You'll find out when you're older. Hopefully with someone who is not Tabitha."

"You can't know that, Devil," Lexie said.

"I know he's not getting near Tiny's girl without a fight. You've got to nip this in the bud, Lex. It won't work out well." Devil grabbed her hand, kissing her knuckles.

"I'm not going to nip it in the bud. You've not seen the two together. Give it time. They'll grow up and grow apart. It's bound to happen." She dropped a kiss to his lips before moving away after ruffling Simon's head.

Devil turned toward them. "No more dirty talk around Simon. Hear me?"

"We hear you." Death and Snake spoke together.

They stayed silent for the next couple of minutes while Devil tried to talk to his son. Death couldn't help but look toward the redhead who was driving his dick to distraction. He'd tried to fuck other women in order to get her out of his mind, but it wasn't working. None of the usual pussy satisfied the craving he had for her. Every time he was balls deep inside a woman Brianna's face would appear in his mind as if by magic. Without a doubt he'd orgasm within seconds of thinking about her. He was fucked, well and truly fucked. There was no way he was taking such a young woman as his. Look what happened to Ashley. She had been young and had ended up without a head for her association with the Chaos Bleeds crew.

"What are you going to be doing about that?" Snake asked, coming to stand beside him.

Glancing to his left, Death stared at Snake, wondering what the fuck he was talking about.

"You and I both know your dick is getting hard for that little hot number over there. What are you going to do about it?"

"I'm not going to do fucking anything about it. She's not my concern." Death made his way toward the pool room Devil had taken the time to install into the club. They were all slowly rebuilding the strip club into something a little classier.

The drugs, for the most part, were completely gone. They still kept to their deals with their suppliers, but none of that shit came through Piston County. Butler was the big surprise within the club. He had cleaned up his act and become one of the living again. There had been a time when Butler would fuck, drink, shoot up, snort, anything to get the high he was searching for.

Death picked up the pool stick then looked at Snake.

"So, you're not going to do anything about that little attraction with Brianna. Do you mind if I take a poke at her? My dick's been wanting some of her for a long time. I wonder if she's red where it matters most."

Death reacted. Dropping the pool stick, he grabbed Snake by the lapels of his leather cut and slammed him against the wall. "You don't touch her, look at her, or even breathe in her direction," Death said, firing out his warning through gritted teeth.

Snake chuckled. "You've got to do something about that, bud. You're fucking horny as hell and can't even stand to have her treated like the other whores." He held his hands up in surrender. "Death, it'll only be a matter of time before one of the other boys claims her. She cleans, cooks, and shit, but she's not an old lady. You need to remember that. If Devil decides she's got to start earning her way the old fashioned way, then it's a free for all on her delightful red pussy."

That was it. Death slammed his fist into Snake's face, taking a lot of delight at the feel of flesh hitting flesh. Snake went down with a thunk. "You keep away from her and tell every other brother that she's taken. She's mine."

He wasn't going to claim her, but he also wasn't going to watch another fucking brother thinking he was going to take her. "Let's play pool."

Snake laughed.

****

Brianna knelt on the floor, scrubbing behind the bar. It was late and a lot of the club had gone to bed, but she couldn't bring herself to sleep when there was such a mess. She hated mess, always had. Dipping the cloth she was using into warm water, she rinsed it out, then set back to work scrubbing the floor.

"Hate mess, absolutely hate it," she said, muttering under her breath.

"What are you doing around here?"

She looked up to see June staring down at her. "Hey." June was one of the main whores at Chaos Bleeds. She had fucked most of the men in the club apart from all the taken members. From what Brianna had heard, June had earned the respect of all the old ladies as she'd not gone after Devil, Ripper, Curse, or Pussy. They were all taken, and they respected the women for not trying to lay claim. "I'm cleaning."

"I can see that. You know there are men here who'd love to get closer to you." June rested her head on her palm. "You wouldn't have to clean floors if you didn't want to."

"No, I'd have to fuck instead."

"Fucking is fun, and it's an excellent way to burn a shit load of calories. Come on, you don't get an orgasm from scrubbing floors."

Brianna took a breath. She didn't get what people saw in sex. Sure, it was a great way to lose weight, but she'd need to be doing it twenty-four seven to even start working on the size of her ass. "I'm happy scrubbing floors."

She'd been around men for the last two years. She was twenty years old and already was happy to be scrubbing floors. Her life had taken a dramatic change when she'd turned eighteen and been sent to her uncle. Brianna shivered recalling the way he'd inspected her body before putting her up for sale. Yeah, she'd worked for the last two years using sex as a means of staying alive. After she'd upset Master, she had been given back to her uncle. She wasn't going to be doing it again, using sex to stay alive.

The Chaos Bleeds crew didn't demand services rendered from her. They needed someone to clean, do laundry, cook, and any other job they wanted to have done. She'd even cleaned the male toilets for them, which had scarred her for life. Men were fucking disgusting.

"Leave her be," Snake said, coming up behind June. "You've got a cock to satisfy."

"But she's so pretty. She doesn't need to be doing this."

Brianne placed the cloth in the bucket and stood. "I like doing this. Cleaning to me is fun." She wiped the sweat from her brow and happened to chance a look behind her. What she saw brought heat to her cheeks. Death was sitting on one of the benches, and between his thighs was a blonde, giving him a blow job. It shouldn't have bothered her. Being in the clubhouse she'd learned the men like to fuck anywhere they could. They didn't care who was watching or what was going on. If they wanted to, they were fucking. She didn't stop her work. Most of the time she continued cleaning while listening to their erotic pants of pleasure.

It had become a little joke to her to see how long she could be in one place before she started seeing sex.

Witnessing Death having his cock sucked, it … hurt. Out of all of the men he'd been one of them who didn't just fuck out in the open, but it could be more than that. She liked the way he looked at her and the way his skin felt against her own when they happened to touch. Brianna wasn't a romantic, far from it. She hated men for the most part, yet Death, he made her want to still believe in men.

He had his fingers in the blonde's hair, who was bobbing up and down on his stick as if her life depended on it. Brianna stared into his eyes, seeing the challenge within his gaze. What did he want from her? Why did he keep looking at her like that? None of it made any sense to her. She barely talked to him or did anything to gain his attention.

Turning away from the scene, she grabbed the bowl and walked toward the kitchen. Devil had all the latest fixings in the kitchen, including two large range cookers. He liked the whole club to be at the clubhouse, and made sure there was more than enough room for everyone.

Someone cleared his throat, and she turned to see Snake leaning against the door frame.

"Do you want me to cook you something?" She'd already cleaned the kitchen until it was shining. The women deserved to cook somewhere special.

"Death's really into redheads."

"Excuse me?"

Snake smiled, walking into the room. He was sporting a black eye, yet it didn't seem to bother him. "If you want Death all you've got to do is show him you're available. He wants you. He keeps denying himself because of what you've been through."

She gripped the handle on the bowl tighter than ever before. There was no need to talk. Words were not necessary right about now.

"I don't know what you're talking about."

"Yes, you do. Out of all the men here, Death's the one man you take notice of. I've seen you, Brianna, I've watched you. I could have grabbed June and started fucking her and you wouldn't really pay attention. Death gets his cock sucked by another whore, and you notice."

"He's never done something like that before. I'm not used to—"

"Bullshit, Brianna. We both know life wasn't worth fucking anything where you were. We got you from that place, and now you're living life. You spend more time cleaning than anything else. The only interest you've ever held is with Death. Do yourself a favor and let yourself go for a second."

Tears filled her eyes. Everyone thought she'd become one of those girls they'd rescued at the strip club. She hadn't, not really. She'd been a private sex slave to a man whose name she didn't know, servicing whoever her Master wanted her to. In the last few months she'd been tested for STDs and STIs. She'd been lucky as she hadn't caught anything. Not many of the other women had been so lucky. She heard several had contracted HIV and AIDS. It was all bad news, but she'd been lucky.

She tipped the water down the sink, wiping out the steel when she was finished.

"I'm going to go to bed," she said.

Brianna went to pass Snake, but he caught her arm, stopping her.

"There's a story with you. We both know there is. Death wants you, and you want Death. There's no room in this club to want something without going to get it."

"You don't know what you're talking about. Let

me go!"

He loosened his hold yet didn't release her.

"Soon women are going to talk about you. Asking about your place. The old ladies have a place in this club. They're taken by a club member. The whores, they know their place is to serve any of us who want them. You, you're making yourself useful by cleaning, yet you take up a room. It'll only be a matter of time before you either become a whore or an old lady."

"Please, let me go."

"Think about it, Brianna. You don't want to end up like June. She's a great woman, but you and I both know she'll never make it as an old lady."

She took a deep breath as he released her. Brianna made her way toward the back of the club. She heard the men and women fucking as she went to her bedroom. It was only a small room, fitting a bed with a small drawer, but it was more than she needed. For the last two years she had nothing to her name. She'd been kept in a cage until her Master wanted to use her. When her Master had finally become bored with her he'd sent her back. Master had wanted her to beg for mercy, to scream, to show something that she truly couldn't do. Ronald, her Uncle Gonzalez's right hand man, had taken her back and beaten her for ruining a good friendship. She sat on the edge of the bed, recalling the pain of his fists on her body. The man she'd been serving was a billionaire, a drug lord, who liked to own things. She'd been another possession. At eighteen years old, she'd been a virgin, ripe for the plucking. He'd taken her under his wing, tutoring her. Even to this day she didn't know his name. She knew him only as Master. Licking her lips, she stared down at her hands. They were locked together.

The tears that she kept locked in all the time spilt down her cheeks. She didn't make a sound. They simply trekked down her face quietly. For so long she'd been quiet, trying to become invisible. The last thing she wanted to do was be noticed.

Chapter Two

"We need a tree," Lexie said, putting a plate in the center of the table. The whole club, members, old ladies, club whores, and kids were sitting around the large table, which was laden with lots of food.

"What?" Devil asked, grabbing a popover from the heaping plate.

"A Christmas tree. We need a large one, decorations as well. I was thinking that we could all spend Christmas here. It has been so long since we were all together. It's way too cold for a barbeque, and we've got plenty of ovens. We can spend Christmas here, all of us." Lexie glanced around the table.

"Oh, I'd like that. We can get presents and everything," Judi said, beaming at Ripper.

"What do you think, Sasha?" Pussy asked, drawing his woman into the conversation.

Her gaze was focused in front of her. Death knew her dog was somewhere. The Labrador had been an investment Pussy had gotten for his blind girl. Death never thought he'd see the day that Pussy was devoted to a woman, especially a blind woman.

"I like it. We've all lost so much. All of us together would be wonderful."

Pussy took her hand, dropping a kiss to her knuckles.

"We can remember Ashley as well."

This was why everyone loved Sasha. She didn't hold a hint of jealousy over Pussy's past relationship with the deceased Ashley.

Ashley had been a club whore who had been adored by the club. She'd been Mia's best friend, Pussy's best friend, and a true asset to the club. To help the club she'd gone with Gonzalez to try to feed information to help them. In return, she got killed by the bastard. Her head had been delivered to them in a box.

"Love you, baby," Pussy said, kissing Sasha's head.

The love between them had Death turning to look at Brianna. She was watching the couple as well. Her hair was pulled back into a ponytail with strands cascading around her face. She looked nervous, maybe even a little envious of what she was looking at. He wondered what she was thinking as she looked at the couple. Did she want that kind of relationship?

"I'm happy for us to remember Ashley," Mia said. Curse gripped the back of her neck, turning her to look at him.

"We'll always remember her."

Mia smiled. For several seconds everyone was quiet. The oven dinged filling the silence. Brianna wiped her plump lips with a napkin before making her way toward the oven.

"What you got cooking?" Lexie asked.

Brianna glanced behind her toward Lexie. "I made several apple pies. I hope that's okay."

Death loved apple pie. He'd eaten loads over the years, but none of them reminded him of his mother's, who'd made the best pies ever.

She was twisting the towel she held, looking toward Lexie.

"Of course it's okay. I hope you made enough. These men are savages when it comes to pies."

"I did."

He watched as she bent over and started to retrieve the pies. Death saw they were not round pies but in a rectangular tray.

"Is this what you were doing first thing this morning?" Judi asked. "I got up and found you elbows deep in flour and butter."

"Yes. I need to make the pastry early so it has plenty of time to chill." The smell from the pies was heaven.

She came back to the table, picking up her knife and fork. He was intrigued even more by her. Who taught her how to cook?

You've not tried them yet. They could be awful.

Death finished eating his food not bothering with a second portion. He was more interested in the pies resting on top of the stove.

Sitting back, he found himself watching Brianna. It wasn't hard to do. She sat on the opposite side of the table about five people down from him. Not once did she look up. She kept her head bowed over her food, eating off her plate. He also noticed, like he did everything about the sexy redhead, that she only ever took one portion for herself. She didn't try to get a second or third. No, there was something different about her. Brianna kept trying to disappear. There was no chance of her hiding from him. He wanted her. The blonde he'd fucked last night hadn't even come close to the kind of desire he had for Brianna.

He was joking if he thought he could get rid of her.

The table was cleared, and Brianna came beside him, reaching over to grab the plates. He didn't make a move to help her. Instead he inhaled the scent coming from her. She smelled like roses. He loved the smell even though he'd never taken the time to appreciate the scent of roses.

She didn't linger like many of the club whores did. When Lexie leaned over Devil, he sank his fingers into her hair, kissing her lips before he released her. Sasha stayed beside Pussy as she'd cause more mess than help. She hated not being able to help. Death had heard her complaining to Pussy about helping, but no one wanted Sasha to hurt herself. The blindness had been caused by her stepfather after he hurt her, throwing her down the stairs. The trauma to her head had caused her blindness.

The stepfather was now dead along, with all their enemies.

The table was cleared, and then the trays of apple pies were brought to the table, along with a large pot of custard. Brianna sat down, but Lexie wouldn't let her.

"You made this, honey, so you can serve."

"I don't mind if you want to serve," Brianna said.

There she went trying to disappear.

"No, you serve," Death said, staring at her.

She stood and began cutting into the pies. Her hand was shaking, but no one said anything. He liked how she served up Simon and the kids first before going around the table.

"Fuck me," Simon said, interrupting the sudden silence.

"Simon!" Lexie snapped out Simon's name. "Language."

"Dad says it all the time," Simon said.

Devil was laughing, and Lexie went bright red. Someone had been getting some hanky-panky a little too close to the kids.

"It's not for you to repeat. I don't want to hear that language from you again." Devil got a slap around the back of the head. It was a light tap, no violence to it. "Help me."

"Son, you'll know when you're older. Don't say that again."

"Pie's good, Brianna," Simon said, sulking.

"Thank you." Her voice was so small. She dished

everyone out, giving him a plate as well. He tried to catch her gaze, but she wouldn't give it. Death took the pie with the custard. Picking up his spoon, he took a bite, and fucking hell, he fell in love. He'd eaten so many pies over the years, but none of them had come close to his mother's concoction that he'd grown up on. No, this pie was better. It was fucking heaven. Looking around the table, he saw the rest of the men agreed. The women loved it as well.

"This is fucking delicious," Snake said.

Brianna offered a smile. That was it. She only smiled. There was no preening or talking about the method. He finished his pie, taking another piece. By the time he was on his fourth slice, the table was clear with only Brianna in the room. She was standing at the sink, cleaning the dishes, putting away the pies that were left over.

He got to his feet, taking his bowl toward her.

"Why are you here?" he asked.

She turned those green eyes toward him. "I'm cleaning up the mess."

"You also helped cook. Leave the dishes. We'll get to them."

"No, you won't. You men say you're going to do the dishes, and then you leave them for us tomorrow morning. I'd rather do the dishes now instead of leaving it to get stuck on the sides." She turned back toward the sink, cleaning the dishes. While he'd been eating his desert he watched her wash, dry, then go back to do the same cycle. Most of the dishes were done.

"This is your way of staying hidden, isn't it?" he asked. Putting his bowl into the sink, he placed his hands on either side of her, trapping her against his body and the sink. She was so tiny compared to him. Her hair was pulled away leaving her neck exposed. He saw her pulse was racing. The desire to suck on her neck was strong. He knew she was clean as he'd taken a personal interest in Brianna's health. She'd been one of the few women who'd come away clean. Brianna was a little bit of a mystery. She didn't talk about her time with Gonzalez. Her silence hadn't bothered him before, but now he wanted to know everything about her.

"I don't mind."

"You clean, getting on your knees on our floors. I saw the toilets were sparkling clean. You're the first woman I know who's not trying to get the boys' attention. You'd rather stay in the sidelines, never getting attention." He leaned down inhaling the sweet scent coming from her. Death could get addicted to that smell. His cock throbbed, pressing against the front of his pants. He wanted inside this hot little piece, but she was too fucking young and had been through hell already.

Her head was bowed down. She wasn't washing the dishes even though her hands were in the water.

"Why?" he asked.

"I don't want to. Is it true what Snake said last night?"

Death froze. "What did Snake say last night?" This was news to him about Snake talking to her. He figured his message had already come across about this woman.

"I'm going to have to become a club whore or an old lady?"

He frowned, listening to her repeat everything that Snake had said.

"Ignore Snake. He doesn't know shit that he's talking about." He couldn't resist anymore and pressed his nose against her neck, inhaling her scent. "You smell so damn good." Wrapping his arms around her waist, he pulled her back against him, holding her close. Her body was so soft, and the need to lose himself inside her was getting harder to resist.

As suddenly as he caught her to him, he released her.

"Where did you learn to cook like that?" he asked.

"My mom. She loved to bake all the time. I learned everything I know from her." She didn't turn to look at him. Brianna stayed still.

"It was good." Death pulled away completely, leaving her alone. He left the kitchen, going in search of Snake. He found June on his travels and ordered her to go and help Brianna. She was currently showing Dick a good time, but it could wait.

June didn't argue, getting up from Dick's lap to go toward the kitchen.

"Cock blocking bastard. Everyone knows Brianna's off limits because Death wants her, and she likes to fucking clean," Dick said.

"I don't care. She doesn't need to do all the shit here. Where's Snake?"

"Outside with Devil and the others sharing a smoke. Fucking prick." Dick got to his feet, cursing.

Death didn't care. Dick could be exactly that, a dick. Not that he was doing much better. Death knew he was being a dick, too, but he wanted the men to stay away from Brianna. He made his way out of the clubhouse to find Snake, Devil, Curse, and Pussy sharing a smoke, laughing and joking. Moving toward them, he slammed Snake to the ground. Death got his name as he caused a shit load of death during his time before he even joined Chaos Bleeds. He liked to kill slowly, meticulously, and was damn good at it.

"You fucking prick."

"I take it you spoke to Brianna?" Snake asked,

laughing.

Death slammed his fist against Snake's face.

Going for another hit, Death didn't get to land a blow as the other three men pulled him off Snake.

"You bastard. You broke my fucking nose," Snake said, getting to his feet.

"What the fuck is going on?" Devil asked.

"I told you to stay away from her, Snake. I fucking warned you. Now you've got her worried about what's going to happen soon."

"Is this about Brianna?" Devil released him, shouting out the question.

"Yeah."

"You laid claim to her yet?"

Pussy and Curse stayed silent while Death answered. "No."

"Then what Snake had to say was right."

"You know what he said to Brianna?" Death asked, turning his glare from Snake toward Devil.

"Who do you think told him to inform her that her time is limited in the club? Most of the women have either become club whores or moved away to make a life for themselves. Brianna has hung around. Don't get me wrong, she's awesome at cleaning, but I got no need for a cleaning lady. I've got prospects wanting to join. Her room is going to be taken soon," Devil said, bringing him back down to earth.

"You knew this was going to happen," Curse said.

"What does Lexie say to this?"

"She's my woman, Death. I say what goes, and she understands. I'm the president. You want to try to take my patch from me, bring it. I'm not stepping down."

"I don't want your patch."

Death couldn't believe what was happening, but

he should have known. Judi had her place because Devil had adopted her as a daughter. Lexie had become his old lady, too. Curse, he didn't bring Mia to the club, but she had her own room, and was now Curse's old lady. The same had happened with Sasha. Pussy had laid claim to her before any other man got a chance at her. Ashley had come to the club and become one of the whores. She shared a man's bed, giving him pleasure.

The thought of anyone touching Brianna filled Death with anger. He'd hurt and kill anyone who thought they could touch what was his. The club had never had to deal with someone like Brianna. She wasn't part of the club. The only thing she did was clean. They didn't need a cleaner.

"No one touches her," Death said. "No one."

"I want her room free by the end of the week. You've got 'til Friday, Death. I was going to talk to her later. You've saved me a job." Devil looked toward the clubhouse. Lexie stood in the doorway, waving at him. Her rounded stomach stood out as she held Elizabeth on her hip. "Fucking woman is going to be the death of me. I've told her not to carry the kids around."

"Ripper's losing his shit, man," Pussy said. "I've never seen him so fucking scared before. I actually think he'd rather be facing a loaded gun than the evidence he's going to be a father."

"Wait until he has a girl. Your world comes crashing down around you. I've got Judi to worry about and Eliza. I don't know what I'm going to do when the boys come to call."

"You'll shoot them," Pussy said. "Nothing keeps a guy's dick in his pants like looking at a loaded gun."

"What are you going to do about Sasha when she has a kid?" Curse asked, chuckling.

"I'm not getting her pregnant. Not yet. I can't

25

share her yet."

Death shook his head. Fuck, he needed to deal with Brianna.

"Take him to the hospital. No one is going to make a move on Brianna. You broke it, you fix it." Devil pointed between them. "I've got my woman to satisfy."

Death watched his president walk toward the clubhouse. "What the fuck, Lex? Put her down."

Lexie didn't put Elizabeth down. When Devil was close enough Death watched him take his daughter from her. "She's not feeling well."

"Come on." They entered the clubhouse together. Devil had his hand on the back of Lexie's neck, leading the way inside. On his other side, Elizabeth lay, holding onto her father.

Cursing, Death made his way toward the car. He always had a key on him. Sliding into the car, he waited for Snake to climb inside.

"You could have forgotten about my nose."

"Shut the fuck up."

It was his own fault.

****

Brianna wiped down the final counter within the kitchen. June stayed to help with the dishes, bitching and moaning. Brianna tried to explain that she didn't need any help with the cleaning. June wouldn't listen to her. She stayed and complained all the time.

Turning around she saw Lexie standing in the kitchen, holding a bundle of clothing. "Elizabeth is sick."

"I can do them." She moved forward about to take the clothing when Lexie stopped her.

"You've got to make a decision, Brianna."

She paused, looking at the old lady of the president of Chaos Bleeds. "Snake talked to me. I know I've got to get out of here or, erm, become a club whore."

Brianna tucked some hair behind her ear. The streets were far more appealing than sleeping with another man for a place to stay. That's what she had done with Master. She became his plaything, and in return she got a roof over her head and food. All she had to do was everything he said.

Cutting off the thought, Brianna looked at the other woman. She was so beautiful even dressed in sweats, with her hair bound up, looking tired from the day's events.

"I'll, erm, I'll get out of here."

There was nothing for her to take with her. The only thing she needed to do was walk out the door. She could do it.

"Have you ever thought of becoming an old lady?" Lexie asked. "You're not going to become a club whore. I can see it in your eyes. You're going to get up and walk out."

Brianna licked her dry lips. "I don't think becoming a club whore or an old lady is for me. I'll be out of your hair." Taking the clothing, she moved to the sink, rinsing out the mess before going toward the wash room.

"Death wants you," Lexie said.

No one had said anything apart from Snake hinting at it. The only closeness they'd come to was that afternoon where he'd sniffed her, trapping her against the sink. She didn't know what to make of him or her response to his closeness. In all of her life she'd never been turned on by a man, not even Master, who used to apply lubrication to be with her.

Pausing, she turned to look at Lexie.

"Don't go anywhere until you know what he wants. I don't know what happened to you, Brianna. I'm not even going to pretend to understand. Judi, she knows what it's like. Her past, it's not the best. We don't want you to go out onto the streets."

Brianna stayed quiet. She'd learned it was best to always stay silent.

"You go onto the streets Death will find you." Lexie stared at her. "This is your time to talk."

"You don't know what Death wants. He doesn't want me. He's been with the other women."

"You're young, and he's not. Trust me on this. Wait."

"Okay." Brianna looked down at the clothing waiting to be washed. "I'll clean these."

"I want you to know that I don't want to do this. Devil runs his club, and I love him."

"I understand."

"Good. I love having you around." Lexie smiled before moving away.

Brianna took the clothes into the washroom and started working on them. While she was working, Dick and another club whore she knew as Amy came inside. She didn't leave the room as she folded the drying clothes.

"Suck me, baby," Dick said.

She kept her back to them, continuing to work.

"What about her?" Amy asked.

"She doesn't care what happens. Suck it."

Brianna had also learned Dick was exactly like his name.

The masculine moans mixed with the sucking sounds filled the room. She ignored them, folding washing. When she finished with the drying, she put the clothes into the basket, and made her way out of the room without even looking in their direction.

She made her way upstairs, knocking on the doors. Most of the time she was directed to come inside.

Several of the men were pounding into the waiting women. None of them stopped as she left their clothing.

"Thank you, Brianna."

Not acknowledging them, she left the room. Was she some kind of freak because sex didn't bother her? She wasn't embarrassed by the men fucking or the naked women. Cleaning was fun to her, something she did to pass the time. With her basket empty she made her way back down to the washroom to find Dick still standing there. He wasn't getting his cock sucked, and the only sign of anything happening was the used condom hanging over the end of the trash bin in the corner.

Ignoring him, she emptied out the washing machine.

"I'll lay claim to you if Death doesn't."

She jerked up, smacking her head on the door of the washing machine as she did. Dick had his arms folded over his chest, staring at her. When she banged her head, he moved toward her.

"Fuck, are you always this clumsy?"

"I'm sorry. I didn't mean to."

He gripped her chin, not hard, and moved her hair out of the way. "You've not cut yourself and you don't need any stitches."

"Thank you."

She stared up at him, waiting for him to leave.

"My offer stands."

"Why?" she asked. Out of all of the men she doubted Dick cared about anyone but himself. He came across as a selfish bastard. Was this to piss Death off? She didn't trust the offer, not one bit.

"You need a man to make a claim or to have all the men use you, or you can leave. I'm offering as I like your cooking, and I like looking at you. My offer stands if Death doesn't make a claim or you want to be with someone different."

"You'll want sex?"

Dick snorted. "Baby, whoever makes a claim to you will want sex. You won't get out of fucking anyone."

He tilted her face this way and that. For some strange reason she wasn't scared of him. The Chaos Bleeds crew was deadly, but none of them hurt the women. They had all risked their lives to save the women on Gonzalez's list.

Before she could stop him, he pressed his lips against hers. She froze, not liking the way he took without asking first.

Instead of fighting him, Brianna had learned to take what was handed to her, and she fisted her hands at her sides, staring at him.

He withdrew staring at her strangely. She held his gaze without backing down.

"If you don't want to be kissed all you have to do is say so." He stormed out of the room leaving her confused.

"I can't say no because I've never been given the option or choice before," she said after he left.

****

"I did it," Lexie said, closing the door, and leaning on it quite heavily.

"Good." Devil pulled his boots off, looking toward her. "Come here."

She went to his open arms, perching on his knee as he locked their fingers together. He gripped the back of her neck, pulling her close to claim her lips. She moaned, appreciating him for brushing his teeth. Lexie didn't mind him smoking, but she hated kissing him with smoker's breath.

"Why are we doing this?" she asked, pulling

away.

"Pushing Brianna and Death together?"

"Yeah. I know you can be romantic but not a matchmaker." She wrapped her arms around his neck as he rubbed at her stomach. Judi was also far along with a rounded stomach of her own. Lexie had watched Ripper caressing her stomach many times.

This was their third child together. Simon had been Lexie's sister's and Devil's child. They were not going to tell Simon the truth. Their son didn't need to know about the crap that happened around his birth. Also, Kayla had been killed by Gonzalez. There was no need to cause any more heartache.

"They're both being stubborn, and I've got to stick with my rules, baby. She's taking up room, and I've got prospects to house."

"Brianna's not stubborn."

"No, she's withdrawn. No one knows anything about her, and she won't talk about it. I think it's unhealthy. Death wants her, and the only time I've ever seen life inside her eyes is when Death is around. They just need a little push, as otherwise she'll spend the rest of her life cleaning, watching as Death takes what little pleasure he can with the club whores. The women will start to question her presence. If Death doesn't take her, someone else will." Devil moved his hand underneath her shirt.

"What if you're wrong?"

"If I was wrong you wouldn't have gone and delivered the message I asked. I know you, Lex. If you truly believed I was wrong, you'd have been like a mother hen protecting her young." Devil pulled her close, claiming her lips once again. "This is what they need. If we're wrong another brother will come forward to make her as his. We're not wrong."

She didn't get time to protest as he took her to the bed and showed her that not only could he be romantic, he could also be downright dirty as well.

Chapter Three

"I can't believe you broke my fucking nose," Snake said. Death sat on the chair in the ward they'd been shown to while Snake sat on the bed. There was a cloth against his nose.

"You can't leave my shit well enough alone."

"If it wasn't for me there wouldn't be any shit for you to deal with. Devil's going to kick her ass out of the club if you don't do something. I was acting as a fucking friend. You're a fucker." Snake kept his head back at the nurse's instructions.

"Keep your nose out of my business. You'll remember I wasn't fucking kidding."

Snake shook his head. "You're a fucking asshole."

Death stayed silent as another nurse appeared. She was a young woman with long raven hair. "You broke your nose?"

"Yeah, that fucker did."

"Do you need me to call the cops? Perhaps put you in a hostel for abused husbands?" The woman smiled at Death. "You did the female world a favor."

"I don't fucking know you," Snake said.

"But I know you. You broke my friend's heart."

Death sat back looking from Snake to the raven haired woman. On her tag he saw the name Jessica.

"I've been with a lot of women with pissed off friends."

"Her name was Lydia. You fucked her about six months ago around the back of the diner. I had to listen to her moan about you." Jessica folded her arms across her chest glaring at him.

Glancing at Snake, Death knew he couldn't remember the woman.

"Unbelievable," Jessica said, clearly seeing the same as him. "You don't remember her at all. God."

She moved toward the side of the ward, grabbing out a pair of rubber gloves. "I don't know what's worse, the fact she remembers you as something more, or you don't even remember her."

"I'd remember you," Snake said.

It was the wrong thing to say. She reached out, gripping the top of his nose. "Yep, it's broken," Jessica said, talking louder over Snake's scream.

"Fuck, woman. This is supposed to be a caring environment."

Jessica glared at him. "I'm very fucking caring right now. She's my friend. You should be lucky you've still got your dick attached."

She grabbed his chart. "A doctor will be down to set your nose."

Death liked this woman. He liked her a hell of a lot for not falling for Snake's shit. Usually, Snake said a shitty assed line and the women were lining up for him. This was not the case.

The curtain stayed open while Jessica handed the file back to the receptionist.

She dropped her pen, and they both watched as she leaned down to grab the pen, revealing the ink at the base of her back.

"Fuck me," Snake said.

"You want to tap that?"

"She's got 'fuck me' written all over her."

Death laughed. "You've got no chance of getting with her. She's loyal to her friend, no one else."

This trip was turning out to be a hell of a lot better than he thought.

Throughout the evening Death caught glimpses of Jessica as she talked to other patients. Snake almost fell off the bed to look at her. The doctor turned out to be a man who fixed Snake's nose up with ease. By the time the doctor was finished it was late, nearing midnight. Death was tired and in need of some sleep. On the way out they found Jessica leaving as well. She had a backpack on her shoulder and was walking toward a car.

"Hey, tell your friend I'm sorry," Snake said, moving toward her.

Jessica looked up, staring at Snake's nose.

"No."

"What?"

"You're not sorry. If you were sorry you'd go and see her yourself. You don't care about her at all." Jessica opened her car door. Death had parked his car three spaces down. It was late, and there were barely any cars in the parking lot.

"I am sorry."

She threw her backpack into the car, turning to look at him.

"You're not. I'm not interested in your excuses. Stay away from Lydia. She's doing much better now. I just can't believe she was so upset that you didn't call." She shrugged. "I guess there's nothing about taste in her decision to sleep with you." Jessica climbed behind the wheel.

"Come on, Snake. I'm freezing my balls off, and you're not going to get near her." Death opened the car, climbing inside.

"That bitch just insulted me."

"I'm sure it won't be the last time a woman insults you. You hurt her friend, and now she knows who you are." Death turned over the ignition ready to get home.

The clubhouse was home.

Glancing over at Snake, Death knew Jessica had

left a lasting mark on him. No one had entered Snake's life, insulted him, hurt him, and left him all in one night.

"Do you need to go and see Mommy and Daddy?" Death asked.

"Fuck you."

"Nope, not fuck me. You want to fuck Jessica. Wait, you can't because she hates you," Death said, laughing.

"You can laugh all you want. Claim Brianna or I'll be fucking her by the end of the week."

Death jerked the car to the side of the road ready to take a hit.

"I'm not going to fucking do it. Just stop your shit about Jessica. I don't need to hear it, okay?"

Staring at Snake, he was tempted to give him another warning. The only problem he had was he'd be the one who would have to go back to the hospital with him. He didn't want to be at the hospital again tonight.

Pulling away from the curb, he made his way toward the clubhouse. Like always the light in the main room was on, but he saw most of the house was dark.

Entering the clubhouse he saw Dick was sitting at the bar. Butler was also with Amy at the table.

June ran toward Snake. "I missed you."

Death was shocked to see Snake hold her away.

"I'm not in the mood." He made his way toward the staircase leading toward the bedrooms.

"What do you mean you're not in the mood?" June asked.

"Exactly what I said." Snake didn't stick around, and Death wasn't in the mood to chat. He made his way up to his room, ready for sleep. He hated hospitals, the smell, the people, all of it. Hospitals were the last place he wanted to be.

Death stopped outside of Brianna's door. It was

one of the smallest rooms in the house. She didn't deserve to be in such a small room.

Pressing a hand to the door, he wondered what she'd think if he walked into the room. *Don't scare her.*

"You're not the only one who wants her," June said from behind him.

He turned toward her. "What?"

"Dick. He made a move on her in the washing room. She didn't respond as far as I could see. I just thought you'd like to know. I don't know what Dick was doing or if he was just messing with shit."

"Are you trying to turn a brother against a brother? No one likes shit like that."

"I'm not trying to do anything," June said. "She's a good girl. Dick wants her, but I don't think he wants her long term. I think he's just messing with you *and* her."

Death was pissed once again. All thoughts of sleep left his mind as he made his way back downstairs.

Going to the bar, he grabbed Dick by his jacket.

"What the fuck were you doing?" Death asked.

Dick laughed. "Who told you? Did Brianna?"

Gritting his teeth, Death growled at him. The last thing he felt right now was human. He was so pissed off and angry at Dick. Death had asked all of the men to leave Brianna alone, but this fuck-head thought he could put his filthy hands on his woman.

She's not yours yet.

You need to claim her first.

"I wanted her to have a choice. I've got a thing for redheads. Who gives a shit what you think? I'm giving her an option."

"Anyone can lay claim to her, Death. We've given you a chance, but Devil's right. She's taking up room when she's not supposed to," Butler said, getting to his feet. "You're both acting like a pair of dicks."

Dick had been one of the men who lived heavily on drink and drugs until Devil demanded they get cleaned.

"Fuck this. I gave her a choice. You're just scared that I might actually have a shot with her. You should have taken her by now."

"Death, let him go. Devil will deal with this in the morning." Butler put a hand on his arm. Death released Dick even though it was the last thing he wanted to do. Marching back upstairs, he stared at Brianna's door.

Grabbing the handle he let himself inside. He found her asleep, curled around a pillow. Throughout the night she'd kicked the blanket off her body, revealing the ratty shirt and shorts she wore. Did she have any clothes of her own?

As he closed the door, a mark on her thigh caught his attention. The mark on her thigh looked similar to what people branded cattle with. What the fuck was that?

She opened her eyes, looking at him. When her brain registered that she wasn't alone she scrambled up in bed, dragging the blanket along with her.

"What are you doing here?" she asked. Her voice wobbled, and all trace of sleep was gone from her eyes. She looked petrified.

"Why do you have a cattle brand on your thigh?"

Her eyes widened. "It's what I was."

"What?"

"I was a piece of cattle. A block of meat. The brand was to make sure I understood that I was nothing."

The words spilling from her lips cut through to his soul.

"Where were you?" he asked.

She shook her head.

He fired questions about her whereabouts, and

she continued to shake her head.

"Why are you keeping this a secret?"

"There's nothing you need to know. I'm nothing special or different."

She held the blanket under her chin. He wasn't going to get anything from her tonight.

"Dick kissed you."

Brianna didn't look away. She stared at him without saying a word.

"Did you like it?"

She shook her head.

"Why didn't you push him away?"

Again, she shook her head.

Cursing, Death looked down at his hands, wondering what the hell he was getting himself into with this woman.

"My uncle," she said.

"What?"

"My parents died, and I had a few weeks left of school. My uncle laid claim, and no one questioned him. I was sent to live with him. After I graduated, he passed me onto a man. That's how I got the brand on my leg. The moment I graduated I was no longer my own person. I was owned."

"Who was your uncle?" Death asked. The moment he found this asshole he was going to kill the fucker, destroy him with his bare hands.

"Ronald. He was Gonzalez's right hand man."

What the fuck?

****

Brianna's heart was racing. Part of her wanted Death to leave her alone but another was afraid. He kept asking questions, so many she couldn't answer. When he asked about Dick, she'd gotten even more scared. She'd learned that if she gave a little something back, the taker usually gave a little, and the pain lessened.

Master had taught her that. If she pleased him and did it willingly, she wouldn't get into so much trouble and it wouldn't hurt.

Licking her dry lips, she stared at him, seeing how tired he was. She didn't want to be with Dick. The truth was she didn't want to be with any man, but Death was the lesser of two evils.

"You were related to that fucker, Ronald?"

She nodded.

"You know he's dead, right?"

"I know." Brianna hadn't mourned Ronald's death. When she'd heard the crew talking about what went down in a place called Fort Wills, she'd been so happy. Unlike a lot of the women she'd only ever been forced to service her master and whoever her master wanted her to serve.

"Don't you care?"

"He was evil."

Death stared at her for a long time.

Neither of them spoke. This was the closest they'd been, apart from when he'd trapped her against the sink. He was a deadly man, and his appearance made him fierce to look at. Death had dark hair that was almost black. Dark brown eyes stared back at her, always assessing her. From the way he looked, she knew he was always thinking, planning.

"You know Devil's going to give you a choice."

After Lexie's visit to her in the kitchen, Brianna knew she didn't have a choice, not really. She nodded in response.

"Then the final decision is up to you," he said. Again, she stayed quiet while he talked. "You can make a choice to either provide for all the brothers or to take just one, and if you don't want either of these you can leave."

"Someone has to want to claim me." She really didn't want to go with Dick. He unnerved her, scared her a little. The kiss he'd given her had been all about possession, ownership. There was something darker to Dick that he kept well hidden from everyone else, but she saw it, and it terrified her.

"I want you," Death said.

Her heart continued to pound. She wasn't ready for this, yet she didn't have a choice.

"Dick also wants you. If you want, I'll beat the shit out of him to prove I'm the better of the two." The smile on his face affected her deeply. She didn't smile back. What was happening wasn't a laughing matter.

"Where will we live?" she asked.

"Here in the clubhouse. I don't have a place of my own. In time I'll get one."

"What does this mean?" She kept the blanket held underneath her chin.

He moved to sit on the bed. She stayed still, liking how close he was. It was strange for her. Most men who came near her unnerved her, forcing her to want to be elsewhere. Death was the first man she actually liked being close to. It made absolutely no sense to her whatsoever.

"It means you'll be mine. You'll sleep in my bed, ride my bike, and ask me about any decisions. You'll become an old lady, like Judi, Lexie, Mia—you know the drill. None of the whores will get to talk back to you."

"But you don't need to keep me as an old lady right? I heard others talking that some men keep a woman just for them. She's not allowed to service any other men?" Why was she questioning him? This was a good thing. Out of all of the available men, Death was the least scary.

Strange, Brianna. His name literally means Death.

She'd heard the other brothers talking. They all talked, and Death was one of the worst men for killing people. Not only did he kill them, he made sure the bodies were never found. Was that why she felt so safe around him? No one had ever gotten the upper hand around him. She'd be safe.

"That kind of thing doesn't happen in Chaos Bleeds anymore. On the road some of the boys would keep a whore for themselves, but that was years ago before we settled down. But I don't want you to be a club whore. I want you to be my old lady."

"Why? You don't even know me."

Shut up, Brianna. It's this, Dick, or the rest of them.

"I know enough about you that I know I want you."

"Will you want sex?" she asked, staring back at him.

"Yes."

Brianna stared at the blanket covering her body.

"It doesn't matter who you pick, they're going to want to have sex."

She knew that.

"I'm going to give you to the end of the week to make a decision." He stood, leaning over her. She tensed for a second as he cupped her cheek. He didn't withdraw from her touch. Death made her look back at him. "I'm going to kiss you right now. You've felt Dick's lips on yours. It's time you felt mine."

There was no way for her to be ready for the riot of sensation that built up inside her. Death's lips were firm but not bruising. Where Dick had taken what he wanted without care, Death took his time, letting her grow accustomed to the feel of his lips on hers.

His tongue glided over her lips asking for access to her mouth. She didn't give it at first, frightened of what it would all mean. The patience he showed allowed her to trust him. Brianna opened her lips slightly, and he plundered her mouth with his tongue. She released the grip on the blanket to grab hold of his arms.

Not once did he release his hold from her cheek. The kiss deepened, and for the first time in her life, Brianna felt warmth spill from the lips of her pussy. She pressed her legs together in an attempt to relieve the building ache inside her.

All too soon he withdrew from her. The kiss was over, yet the heat remained.

"Think about that while you're making your decision. I've done a lot of bad shit in my time, Brianna. I've killed, hurt, and maimed, but I've never take a woman against her will. I will not force you, rape you. When we're together I want you to be there every single step of the way. I'll be patient, but I'll not wait around forever." He stroked his thumb across her cheek before leaving her alone.

She stared at the closed door wondering what the hell she was to do. Her lips tingled, and her body felt all achy like she needed to be touched or stroked. Staring around her small room, she knew the choice she needed to make.

****

The following day Devil sat at the head of the large table in the Chaos Bleeds meeting room, looking over the prices for a blasted Christmas tree. He wasn't in the mood to be dealing with all this festive crap, but seeing the look of joy on Judi's and Lexie's faces, he knew he couldn't deny them a Christmas to be proud of. He called for a club meeting, and all he was doing was waiting for the men to enter the room. Snake was the first man to enter. He looked like shit with bruises along either side of his nose.

Ripper, Curse, and Pussy filed in together, taking seats around the large table. This was the room where they took votes, made plans, and settled scores.

Death and Dick were two of the last to arrive. They took their seats glaring at each other.

"What's the meeting being called for, boss?" Pussy asked, looking way too happy. Married life suited him, and even being married to Sasha suited him, which surprised the fuck out of Devil.

"We've got to decide upon a tree. Lexie gave me all of this shit to decide. It's my club, and we're to decide what tree we get." This was their first order of business. Since he'd been with Lexie he celebrated Christmas at home with a few of the brothers stopping by. This year was different. They had all lost parts of themselves because of Gonzalez. Devil knew he was changed. Transporting young girls had broken a part of him that he'd never get back. In all of his years of being a biker, he'd never once been pushed into dealing in underage girls. He'd dealt in guns and drugs but never that. It was hard at times when he had Elizabeth in his arms, and he stared at Judi. They were his girls. Judi wasn't his by blood, but she was his. He'd laid claim to her, adopted her, and she had become the club princess. If anyone touched his daughter, he'd fucking kill them. Everything he despised he'd done because of the threat Gonzalez posed. He wasn't going to let that happen. Chaos Bleeds were going to be stronger for it. Piston County was going to be theirs, and there wouldn't be any threat in the future. He'd take the lead to make sure the club and his boys were protected.

"You're fucking serious?" Dick asked. "You've called us all in for a fucking tree?"

"Watch your fucking mouth. I heard about you, you little shit. This is what my woman wants. She takes care of the club."

"Sasha's looking forward to it, too. I was going to take her away for Christmas, but she's happy to stay here." Pussy reached out to grab the list from him before turning to look at Dick. "You've got to have a woman who wants you for more than your dick to understand. Oh, you've also got to have more about you. You, Dick, you're just a dick."

No one argued with Pussy's assessment. Devil glared at Dick, who kept his fucking mouth shut. He'd be talking with him all too soon.

"The fir one with fake snow sounds good," Pussy said. He passed the page around the club, while each man added in their input. Devil was going to spank Lexie's ass for making him do this. There wasn't anything he wouldn't do for her. He wondered if Lexie had figured that out yet. His love for her had only gotten stronger over the years, even with her visiting Eva. How could he deny her anything?

"In the new year we're going to have to start organizing women for the strip club. We all want a new name, fresh start, none of the shit that went down, we want it all gone." He looked toward Vincent. "Are you still okay to work it?"

"I'm fine with that. We set down the ground rules, and the boys can help out where they can."

"No drugs," Butler said, speaking up. "We keep the drugs out of it."

Devil nodded. He was proud of Butler for taking a new lease on life.

"I'm in agreement with that," Curse said. "Drugs are out of it. We're no longer controlled by it. We're all clean."

The boys nodded in agreement. They had five men still in rehab dealing with their addictions. Devil had given all the men an ultimatum, get clean or get out of the club. Gonzalez had stepped up his game, and Devil hadn't been about to be at the mercy of the bastard.

"No dealing from the women either. They're checked regularly," Ripper said.

"No old ladies in the club," Pussy said. "I know I've got no worries from Sasha, but I don't want the women thinking we're going to stray."

"I'm not keeping Judi away," Ripper said. "She trusts me. There's no woman I want more than her."

"Me neither," Curse said. "I'm talking about Mia."

"I gathered." Devil said. He didn't need to add that he wouldn't stray from Lexie. There was no way he'd risk losing his woman for a piece of pussy. She was all he needed. "Okay, we'll handle the hiring of the women. Also, we'll deal with the running of the club, helping you out, Vincent."

"I don't care what you need to do. I'm with you, Devil. You know me. I've already talked to Phoebe, and she's happy with it. I wonder if she hopes I'll stray." He made a joke. The men chuckled. They all knew Vincent was loyal to his woman. No one could get him to stray. On the night of his bachelor party, Devil tried to get him to have one night of freedom to remember what free pussy was all about. He wouldn't do it. Devil remembered Vincent getting angry, telling him it was supposed to be about fun. Cheating, to Vincent, wasn't about fun. They all also knew that Vincent was an insatiable man. He'd stop what he was doing and hunt

Phoebe out just to fuck her. It was probably why Phoebe became a stay-at-home mom.

"What's going on with Brianna?" Snake asked, drawing the conversation to the topic Devil really didn't want to discuss.

"She's been given her options. I've given her a week to make a choice."

"It's a bit harsh, don't you think?" Pussy asked. "It is Christmas."

"Ronald was her uncle," Death said.

"What?" All the men snapped, turning to look at Death.

"I talked to her last night. Her parents died and she needed to finish school, so they sent her to Ronald without question. Once she finished school, he passed her onto another man who owned her."

Devil saw this news pissed Death off.

"I didn't ask any more questions. Even being related to the fuckers didn't help her."

"No, but now we've got to know where she came from and if someone's going to try to make a play for her," Dick said.

"You mean like you did last night?" Death glared, facing Dick.

"No one said she was off limits. I saw an opportunity, and I fucking took it."

Death got to his feet at the same time as Dick.

Devil wasn't in the mood to replace all of the furniture in his office. Christmas was already going to cost him plenty.

"Sit the fuck down," he said.

Both men slowly lowered themselves into the chair, neither one looking happy about it.

"Whoever comes around Brianna doesn't want to be with them. She's fucking terrified but hides it," Death said.

"I agree." Curse spoke up this time as did Ripper.

"Judi has talked about her. She believes Brianna's learned to be obedient. We've all watched the redhead. There's nothing right about her. She doesn't care about the sex going on. In fact, she does everything to ignore everyone and to stay hidden."

Devil nodded. "We'll deal with Brianna in time and if any shit comes from her."

They talked about setting drug runs back up, but Devil decided against going straight into drug runs.

"We've got a town to protect. Jerry's no longer with us. Gonzalez is out. We've got to find the people who want the best for the town and not someone who is going to fucking break the town for a quick buck," Devil said. His biggest issues were the cops who wanted to earn money on the side. They could be dangerous for the town and for his club.

"I can give Whizz a call and ask him to look at the men currently on the force," Pussy said. "We got on quite well."

"Be careful. Tiny won't like it," Devil said.

"You're still going to stay away from Fort Wills and Tiny?" Death asked.

"He insulted us. We've caused each other more trouble than not. I'm not going to start up relations again. We're fucking finished."

"Simon doesn't think so," Pussy said, speaking up.

Devil shot him a glare.

"What? Anyone who's listening can hear your son has got a hard-on for Tabitha. Have we all forgotten who Tabitha is? Right, she's Tiny's daughter." Pussy looked around the table.

"First, my son is too fucking young to have a

hard-on for anything. Give it time and he'll forget about her. He's not your concern."

Pussy stared back at him looking doubtful.

Once everything was dealt with, Devil dismissed the club but demanded that Dick stay behind.

When the door was closed, he stared down the table at Dick. He was an asshole to the core, but he was also a great man, a loyal man.

"What the fuck are you doing with Brianna?" Devil asked.

"I gave her a choice. I didn't realize it was only for Death to make a claim."

"You've not showed any interest before."

"I've not showed interest because I was giving her time. If she wants Death, fine. If not, I'm happy to take her."

"Back away from her, Dick, unless your claim is real. You've never showed any signs of wanting her before at all. I'm not in the mood for your games. If you're just fucking with Death, don't," Devil said. Whatever had happened to Brianna, Dick didn't have the skill to handle it. He was a selfish bastard. Anyone could see it, but Dick was known for getting a kick out of pissing brothers off. His sudden interest in Brianna could be to piss Death off.

"Is this a direct order or an advisory?"

"You don't love her, and you're not looking at long term. Death wants her. Leave her to him. I'm not interested in paying for any cleanup between the two of you." Death and Dick fighting would be a problem for the club.

"What makes you think he's better than me?" Dick asked.

"I don't. You're trying to cause shit for Death. Two of my men at each other's throats is not what I want to be dealing with. Get your kicks elsewhere, Dick. I mean it."

"Death's easy when it comes to Brianna."

"You're fucking everything that walks around. Don't fucking argue with me, Dick. You're not going to like it."

"Fine, can I go?" Dick asked.

"Yes."

Alone, Devil rested his head against the back of his chair.

Lexie appeared in the doorway. "Am I allowed to enter this domain?" she asked.

He pulled away from the table, tapping his lap. "I've always got room for you."

She walked toward him, giving him time to admire her curves. They were generous. He couldn't wait to get his hands on her.

"What's going on? You look stressed."

"Dick's being an asshole and trying to make a claim on Brianna. I believe the bastard is trying to get his kicks out of causing problems in the club." Lexie tensed in his arms. "Don't worry. I've warned him. I've not got any interest in dealing with brothers fighting over a woman."

"I never knew he had a thing for her."

"He doesn't. Dick will take what he wants and spit her back out. She'd be more scarred by the end of it."

"Has he always been like this?"

"From the very beginning. Dick was different when he was on drugs, but before the drugs, this is exactly what he was like. Whatever woman truly catches his eye has got some work on her hands. He's a possessive bastard when he starts."

She rested her head against his body. "I love you,

Devil."

"I love you, too, baby, more than you'll ever realize."

Chapter Four

The delivery of the tree came two days later, and Death along with several of the brothers was dragging it into the house. Lexie was barking out orders of where she wanted it to go. Out of the corner of his eye he saw Brianna waiting with a dustpan and brush to clean up the pine needles. He wished he understood where her obsessive need for cleaning came. Ever since he'd gone into her bedroom she'd done everything to avoid him. He also noticed she didn't sit and eat with them anymore, either.

She'd taken a step back from everything.

Death wasn't going to allow her to hide for much longer. He'd given her a couple of days, and he wasn't going to wait much longer. What he told her hadn't been a lie. He wouldn't force her to be with him.

The last couple of nights he'd brought himself off with the image of her spread out before him waiting for his pleasure. He'd not told any of the brothers about the brand he'd seen on her thigh. She would have to see it every day to get dressed. What was it like for her to see the brand?

Death didn't know what to make of it himself. Thinking about the brand he decided to go and visit the man who handled their ink. If he could get it to look like something else, she might be able to forget about the past.

"There in the corner by the window," Lexie said, pulling his attention back to what he was doing.

"For fuck's sake, Lex, pick a spot," Devil said.

"I've picked. In the corner."

They placed the tree in the corner. It was huge but would look amazing when all the decorations and lights were on it.

Glancing around him he saw the couples were wrapped around each other looking at the tree. Ripper stood behind Judi with his hands on her stomach. Devil held Lexie's neck as they stared up. Curse rested his head on Mia's, and Pussy looked at his own woman. For the first time ever Death saw the sadness in Pussy's eyes.

"I wish you could see it, baby," he said.

Death was close enough to hear him talking to the woman.

"I'm sorry." She always apologized for her eyesight.

"Don't be sorry." Pussy kissed her temple. "It's a pretty big tree. It's well over seven feet tall. We'll have to get a ladder to put the angel on top." Pussy stroked her hair as he began to tell her about the tree. "It's a giant green fir tree, baby. I begged for one covered in fake snow, but this got the vote."

"It's a traditional tree?" Sasha asked.

"Yeah."

"Fake snow would have looked awesome."

"When we decorate it I'll describe it to you then. I'm not good at this, baby. All I've got is it's big and green."

Sasha giggled, reaching up to touch Pussy's cheek. "It's perfect."

Glancing behind him, Death saw Brianna staring up at the tree with tears in her eyes. It was one of the first raw emotions he'd seen her have. She hadn't moved but stared at the tree. Suddenly, she turned and walked back toward the kitchen.

Not staying around to watch the rest of the club, he followed her into the kitchen, concerned. She was pacing up and down shaking her hands out.

"Stop it, Brianna, stop it," she said.

"What's going on?" he asked.

She jerked around, looking at him. The tears were falling down her cheeks. He reacted, stepping in close to her. Brianna took a step back, but he wouldn't let her leave. He snagged her hand pulling her close. She fought him. Wrapping his arms around her, he wouldn't let her go. He held her tight to him.

"It's okay. I'm here."

Brianna shook without a sound coming out of her. Her arms didn't go around him. They stayed still, not touching him anymore than she had to.

"I'm not going to let you go. I'm not going to let anything hurt you." Resting his head on her neck, he didn't pull away or stop. The scent of roses invaded his senses. His cock hardened at the softness of her body. When her silent sobbing stopped, he still didn't let her go.

Slowly, he felt her arms start to close around him. Brianna didn't push him away. She held onto him. Death felt the victory course through his body. There was no way he was going to let Dick get near her. She was all his, and he wasn't going to let her go.

"I've got you."

"I'm so sorry," she said.

Pulling away, he cupped her face. She didn't release him, holding onto his waist.

"You've got nothing to feel sorry about." He wiped the tears from under her eyes. It had been months since they'd taken her away from hell. She'd stayed at the clubhouse, cleaning, cooking, and not once giving away any part of herself. This felt new to Death. He'd witnessed the pain within her eyes.

"My family died at Christmas. The tree, it brought everything back."

"You don't have to tell me why you cried. I'm not going to stop you from feeling, Brianna." He stared down into her green eyes. She was so young and had the whole world at her fingertips.

You want her for your own.

He'd never hurt her. Death would go out of his way to care for her.

"I've not cried in such a long time."

"You can cry whenever you want. Why do you cry silently?"

"I wasn't allowed to be heard, Death. No one wants to listen to a thing cry."

His temper rose. "You're not a thing." Taking her hand away from him, he pressed her palm to her chest. "You're a living, breathing person. Forget him, Brianna. Learn to live. Whatever that fucker did to you, he's not going to come for you."

"You don't know that."

"He gave you back to your uncle." Death gripped her chin, forcing her to look at him. She didn't fight him, not once. "I'll be here to take him out if he comes for you. I'm not going to let you go."

"Why?"

"Because I want you. I'm going to wait until you're ready to give me what I want. No one is ever going to take you from me, Brianna." He leaned down, breathing her in. When he could stand it no longer, he claimed her lips, tasting her again.

She whimpered. Her hands went from his waist up to his arms. He expected her to push him away. Brianna gripped him tighter, kissing him back. Her response to him thrilled him to the core. Moving her back to the wall, he sank his fingers into her hair. The red length was left wild around her. He held her head as he took possession of her lips. Running his tongue along her bottom lip, he eased his way inside, waiting for her to open up in response.

"You're so fucking beautiful," he said in between kisses. Her eyes were closed and her cheeks flushed. She was responding to him. Death pulled away to stare into her eyes. "Did you want my kiss?"

"Yes."

This was all new territory.

"Show me," he said.

"What?"

"Show me you want my kiss."

He'd never have her mistaking his intentions. Brianna was going to be part of this relationship equally.

She stared at his chest for several seconds. Her hands were still lying on his arms. Death waited to see what she'd do. He saw the hard buds of her nipples pressing against the shirt she wore.

Was she wet? He was desperate to find out yet waited. All good things came to those who waited.

Slowly, she glided her hands up his arms going to his neck. She rested her fingers against the pulse beside his neck. Her gaze stayed on her hands where they lay before gliding around his neck. She went to her toes drawing his head down to hers. Death didn't make her fight for his lips.

He made sure she pulled him down. At first she pressed her lips to his, smashing them together. The action was awkward. Was this what Ripper had gone through? Cutting the thought off, he knew Brianna was different from Judi.

They were two different women with two different paths. Neither of them were the same kind of woman.

Her other hand circled his neck, and she finally let go. She didn't press hard but claimed his lips in a proper kiss. His cock tightened to the point of pain. The hard buds of her nipples pressed against his chest.

Death gripped her ass drawing her close to him. She moaned, deepening the kiss, plunging her tongue into his mouth. The kiss went from sweet to naughty in a matter of seconds. He thrust his cock against her stomach, wanting to sink inside her tight cunt.

"Death," she said, whimpering.

"I know, baby. I know." He squeezed her ass one final time then pulled away. Death took her hands from around his body and held them out in front of them.

"What are you doing?" she asked.

"I'm not going to take you, Brianna. I want you. You've got 'til Friday to make a decision." He reached out, stroking her cheek.

She didn't say anything and he turned away, going back out toward the main part of the club. Judi and Lexie were looking through boxes of decorations.

Grabbing his jacket from the chair he made his way out toward the door.

"Where are you going?" Snake asked. June was sat beside him, stroking his leg showing Snake what she wanted.

"I'm going out for a ride."

"I'm coming."

Snake got up from the sofa and followed him outside.

"Should you be riding with a broken nose?"

"I don't give a fuck. I need to get out of here." They climbed on their bikes. He didn't want the confines of a helmet, and he saw Snake didn't even bother with a helmet either. They rode out of the compound. It was cold out, and the roads had been treated because of the snow. The sides of the roads had mounds of snow. The festive season was present everywhere they went. Death drove toward town, wanting some time away from the club and the women.

Snake parked his bike next to Death's. Entering the diner, he took a seat near the window. The diner wasn't busy, and they were served within moments by one of the women Mia had spoken with. When they'd first come to Piston County, they'd struggled to be served. The years were passing quickly, and more of the locals were accepting them within the town.

"Thank fuck for that," Snake said. "I didn't think we were going to get served. I sure miss Mia working here."

Curse no longer wanted Mia working the multiple jobs she was once doing. The last Death heard Mia was studying for her degree in business or some shit like that.

"Why the need for a ride?" Snake asked.

"Brianna."

The waitress came to the table. Death saw the name tag read Charlie.

"Thanks, love," Snake said, winking at her.

She didn't respond, pouring the coffee into the cup. He saw she was already married.

When they were alone once again, Snake fired another question at him about Brianna.

"Why are you taking your time? She's there to be taken."

"Brianna isn't like every other woman." Death sipped at the coffee, grabbing the sugar and cream resting in the basket on the table.

"She's not like every other woman, but that doesn't mean you've got to wait around for her. June told me what Dick did. Why don't you leave her in the hands of someone else?"

"You warned her about the shit that's about to happen and now you're advising me to leave her to Dick? That fucker would scar her for life."

"Do you really think she's not scarred already?"

Snake asked. "We all see she's fucked over."

"She's not fucked over." Brianna was still a woman underneath all the pain she'd been through. There was nothing wrong with her. She wasn't broken inside or fucked over. The biggest problem with Brianna was her training. He was going to make sure to smash down all of her training until the only thing left was the real woman within. It would take time, but he didn't care. She deserved to have someone who cared about her.

"Only you would pick a woman who's a challenge. Fucking crazy if you ask me," Snake said.

"I'm not asking you."

****

Brianna touched her lips from where Death had kissed her. Her whole body ached once again. Wetness flooded her pussy, and it was all because of him. Licking her lips she was sure she could still taste him.

Moving away from the wall, she walked toward the fridge grabbing out the four chickens stored there. With the whole club within one space required her to cook a lot more for all of the men.

She set about preparing the chickens, washing them before stuffing them with a dressing she'd made earlier. Seasoning the chickens, she poured a little oil on each, and placed each chicken within the oven.

"Can I help?"

Brianna turned to see Judi standing in the doorway. Her arms were folded underneath her breasts.

"I've got it covered if you want to go back to decorating," Brianna said.

Judi wrinkled her nose. "I can't. Lexie's having a fit about the decorations. This is the first Christmas spent in the club. The decorations are crap. We're going to have to go shopping to finish the tree. It's a shame as I really want to see that monster all lit up looking beautiful."

"You can peel the carrots and parsnips," Brianna said.

She watched Judi hobble toward the kitchen counter where she'd put the vegetables. The pots were large enough to feed the crowd.

Moving toward the sink, Brianna started to peel the potatoes. She didn't say anything, and the silence seemed strange to her. During her months at the clubhouse she'd not taken the time to talk to anyone.

"Are you always this quiet?" Judi asked.

"I was just thinking I should talk, but I don't know what to talk about."

"Talk about anything. It helps to just talk."

"I've got nothing to say." Brianna placed the potatoes into a large pot. In no time her hands were wrinkly from having her hands in the water for so long.

"I was a whore at a young age," Judi said, startling Brianna.

Turning toward the other woman, she saw Judi was smiling back at her.

"I'm not lying to you. I was a whore. I ended up living with my aunt who sold me to a pimp, and he sold me out to men. Devil and the boys saved me when I was seventeen. They saved me."

There was no pain in Judi's eyes as she smiled back at Brianna.

"I, erm, I didn't know."

"It's all in the past. I've not given it much thought in a long time." She stopped peeling to touch her stomach. "What happened doesn't define me. I'm going to be a damn good mom to my kid."

"Does Ripper know what happened?" Brianna asked.

"He was there when I was being beaten by a

pimp. Ripper knows everything about me. There are no secrets between us. I'm just telling you so you know it's easy to talk about once you allow yourself to start talking."

Brianna went back to the potatoes, peeling them.

"You can talk to me or you can talk to Death," Judi said.

"There's not a lot to talk about. Not really."

"What happened to you shouldn't have happened."

Brianna finished peeling the last potato before moving to the counter where Judi stood. She took out each potato cutting them up before putting them in a separate saucepan.

"I don't even know the man's name," she said. "I was only ever allowed to call him Master. He's all I've ever known." Brianna stopped talking as she took each potato and cut them up before adding to another pot then grabbing another potato. "It wasn't all bad. There were times it was hard, especially when he had friends." She stopped talking as she turned to look at Judi. "He was my first. I'd not had sex or done anything until I was with him."

"He trained you?"

She nodded. "He trained me to take it without complaining. I learned it was a lot easier to just let it happen. The sooner I let it happen, the easier it was. It would be over. Providing I gave him what he wanted, I was left alone."

"It wasn't always like that?"

"No, sometimes he liked to hurt. He liked to provoke me until I couldn't stay silent or still. It wasn't always like that. I think he wanted me to fight him at times." Brianna shrugged. "My time with him wasn't all bad. I didn't end up like a lot of those girls that Devil and the crew saved."

Judi didn't say anything for a long time. Brianna continued to cut the potatoes, her thoughts going back to Death and the kiss he'd asked for.

He was the first man to ask her to prove she wanted him. When he pulled away from her, she'd not wanted it to end.

"What do you think of Death?" Judi asked.

"I like him. He's the first man I've ever felt comfortable with."

"What about Dick?"

Brianna stopped, turning to look at Judi. "He kissed me."

"Did the kiss make you feel anything?"

"No. I stayed still because I know it'll be easier if I don't do anything."

"You've got to stop acting like you're still in *his* home. This is the clubhouse, Brianna. Wake up, snap out of the control he has. You're away from *his* control. You're not your own person while you're still acting like pain is going to come." Judi placed a hand on her shoulder. "It's what I did, and I was suddenly able to breathe easier. You're different. I didn't have just one man to satisfy. I was ordered to satisfy an abundance of men."

Brianna didn't correct Judi on her assumption she'd only been with one man. Master did have a lot of friends he liked to share her with. He liked to brag about how he owned a woman who didn't do anything on her own.

Brianna hated the control he had over her. Judi was right. She was acting like she was still with Master when she wasn't.

Freedom.

She was free, and she needed to start realizing it.

They finished doing the vegetables. The scent of chicken filled the air, making her mouth water and her stomach growl. Mia walked into the kitchen and got stuck in as well.

"What are we doing?" Mia asked.

"Roast chicken." Judi answered as Brianna was basting the meat.

They were joined by Lexie. "I feel sorry for Sasha, I really do."

"Why?" Judi asked. "Pussy adores her."

"Nothing. He's just being classic Pussy winding Devil up with Simon." Lexie took a carrot stick, sitting at the table.

Brianna liked the family feel the women were showing.

"Is it true about Simon and Tabitha?" Mia asked, washing out the mugs to make drinks.

Lexie had gone to visit Eva three weekends ago. While she'd been gone Devil had been checking his cell phone every few minutes waiting for her call. Brianna had watched the worry on the president's face as he waited for his woman to come back home.

"They're friends. I don't see it being a concern when they get older. Simon will find other girls, and Tabitha will be around other boys. I don't see a problem," Lexie said.

"What if it is?" Judi asked, taking a seat over from her. "Simon's stubborn. I saw him looking through the catalogue to send her a gift."

"He's not old enough to have anything. They're friends. I can't believe you're all worried. Devil's just worried. This thing with Tiny and their clubs, it's still raw."

Brianna placed the potatoes in the oven to roast. She tucked hair behind her ear and glanced over at the woman.

"Have you thought about what I said?" Lexie asked.

She nodded. "Death, he's offered me a place by his side." All the women were looking at her.

"Are you going to take it?" Lexie snagged another carrot stick, resting a hand on her swollen stomach. Even heavily pregnant the woman was sexy as hell. Brianna understood why Devil was so possessive and protective of her.

"I don't know."

"Death's a good man, Brianna. He'd give you a good life," Judi said.

There was a time she'd have been able to converse with these women easily. Ronald and Master had taken away that ease. She now didn't have a clue what to do or say. They were different women from her, normal women. They loved their husbands and the club. Could she bring herself to become part of the world once again?

June chose that moment to enter with Dick following behind her. He looked toward her, wrapping his arms around June's waist and pulling her close. There was no jealousy inside her at his actions. When she'd seen Death getting a blow job from one of the other women, she'd been hurt. Could she handle the thought of him being elsewhere?

"I'm going to clean."

She didn't make any more excuses and made her way out of the room. Death being with other people bothered her.

****

"Get out," Lexie said, glaring at Dick. He was living up to his name in more ways than one. June did as she was ordered. She was one of the club whores whom

Lexie actually respected. The other woman hadn't tried to make a play at her man, but if she did, Lexie was going to hurt the bitch.

Several club whores *had* tried to make a play for her man, but now all of them stayed well clear of Devil.

"Do you think she's going to go with Death?" Mia asked, looking toward where Brianna had escaped.

"She is," Judi said. "There's something between them. It's going to take a little time for her to get out of the habits she's trained herself to do in order to survive. Death is perfect for her."

Lexie sat back, thinking about it. "Death cares about her. He won't let anyone hurt her."

"Do you really think pushing the issue is wise?" Mia asked.

Devil had allowed her to confide in the other old ladies about their plan with Brianna and Death. They were all trying to bring the couple together. She'd watched them for the last couple of weeks. The attraction between them was clear to see. Death and Brianna deserved to have some kind of happiness. What Devil had warned her of the fact he couldn't allow Brianna to stay in the club without someone making a claim. If Death didn't make a claim then Brianna had to make a choice. Lexie hoped she'd gotten it right with Brianna and Death. The two would be so wonderful together.

Chapter Five

Death was listening to Snake complain about his nose when Jessica walked into the diner. She was wearing her nurse's uniform, and she made to pass them. When she saw them sat at the table, she stopped to give him a smile.

"Hello." Her gaze turned to Snake. She lost her smile. "I see your nose is on the mend."

"Sit with us," Snake said, snagging her hand. Jessica pulled out of his hold.

"I don't think so. I'm meeting Lydia in a moment."

She passed their table going toward the back. Death watched as she took a seat, grabbing the menu.

"Do you want to leave?" Death asked.

"Fuck no. I want to see what the bitch looks like."

"You really can't remember fucking her?"

"No. I can't." Snake took a long drink of his coffee, taking a fry from his plate. They had ordered burgers with all the trimmings. Death couldn't stop thinking about Brianna and the feel of her lips as she kissed him back. Her response had been heady, and he didn't want it to end.

"What the fuck's got a smile on your face?" Snake asked, growling out the words.

"You've got a hard-on for Jessica, and you can't do fuck all about it because you've fucked her friend."

"Bite me, Death. Seriously, I'm not in the mood. You've broken my nose and now you're fucking with my head as well."

Still laughing, Death turned toward the front of the diner as the door opened. Cool air blew through the whole of the diner, and the woman closed the door. She had brown hair and was completely slender whereas

Jessica was curvy.

Death watched Jessica wave toward her friend.

The look of horror on Snake's face was easy to see. Lydia stopped by their table, smiling at Snake.

"Hey, Snake," she said.

"Hey."

He didn't understand the horror on Snake's face.

"Hey," Death said, interrupting as Snake made no move to make introductions between them.

"Hello." Lydia shook his hand.

"I'm Death."

"I know who you are. I was hoping to hear from you, Snake."

"Your friend is waiting," Snake said, glaring at the woman.

Lydia's cheeks went red. "Okay, well, it was nice to see you again."

Snake didn't say anything.

When they were alone, Death took a bite out of his burger.

"Why do you look disgusted?" Death asked, talking with mouthfuls of food. "Do you remember her?"

"She's a fucking bunny boiler. A fucking animal in bed and not in the best way."

"Huh?" Death looked toward Lydia.

He caught Jessica glancing toward the table.

"Okay, she's a screamer, biter, and she fucking hits during sex. I had to hold her down. There is nothing sane about that bitch." Snake shuddered.

Death didn't even recognize her. "You must have fucked her elsewhere."

"The first time was around the back of the diner. She was fine. We went back to her place and she turned into a lunatic. Eat up, I want out of here."

Death finished off his burger, enjoying how

uncomfortable Snake looked. It served the bastard right to not have life go his way. The woman he clearly wanted wasn't going to let him get near her. The loyalty between the two women wasn't as strong as Mia and Ashley's. He saw they were only friends. Jessica kept looking toward Snake.

Death wondered what was going on inside her head.

Once they finished their meal, Death pulled out notes and left them on the table, including a big tip for Charlie.

They were on their bikes heading back to the clubhouse in no time. As they pulled up in front of the clubhouse he found Devil outside smoking. Butler was standing with him but not smoking.

Death stopped with Snake to talk with the two men.

"We're going out tomorrow for new decorations. You're going as well," Devil said.

"Is that an order?" This came from Snake.

"What the fuck is it with you all questioning me? Yeah, it's a fucking order." Devil threw his cigarette to the ground, storming back inside the clubhouse.

Butler was laughing. "We've got a Christmas list to get. The women are seriously taking over this year. There's no way we can get away from this. I know. I've fucking tried." He headed back into the clubhouse.

Death had taken the list from the man and saw it was indeed a long list. "Baubles, tinsel, lights."

"We're all turning into fucking pussies for these women." Snake walked back inside. June was at the counter. Death watched him grab her around the waist and haul her upstairs.

Brianna was nowhere in sight, and he took a seat at the bar. Judi was drinking a soda.

"Where's Ripper?" Death asked, taking a seat.

"He's gone to the store. We ran out of chocolate ice cream, and I'm needing some."

"Should have called me, honey. I'd have stopped by the store for you on the way back." He ruffled her hair, and she batted his hand away.

"I'm not a young girl anymore, Death." She pulled the band from her hair, pulling her hair back together and putting the length back up.

"I know. You're bringing another younger one into the world. How are you handling it?"

Lexie never handled the early stages of pregnancy well. She tended to need a lot of sleep as she got exhausted and vomited a lot.

"I'm handling it fine." Judi pressed a hand to her stomach. "I'm so excited."

He chuckled at the glow on her face.

"I spoke with Brianna today."

Death stared back at her.

"You've got to get through to her. The woman she once was is there, waiting to come out. I promise you, Death, she's there."

"What do you mean?"

He listened as she talked about what she had learned about Brianna. "She only knows him as Master?"

"Yeah, it's fucking crazy." Judi sipped at her drink. "She wants you, Death. Take her, make a claim."

"I've given her 'til Friday to make a decision."

"Who gives a fuck about Friday? Don't make her wait for you. Spend time with her. She'll open right up with the right man."

"How do you know?" he asked.

She smiled. "It's what happened between Ripper and me. He was the man for me, and I know I can be myself around him."

Ripper chose that moment to walk inside the clubhouse carrying a tub of ice cream. Judi jumped down from the stool and moved toward her husband.

Death watched from his seat at the bar as the two embraced. Ripper had been through hell to prove his love for Judi. Devil had wanted to kill the man for touching her. The whole of the club had wanted to hurt him for touching her. Judi had been and still was the club princess. No brother should have touched her. The love between the two was what kept Ripper breathing.

He knew Devil still held a gun ready to take Ripper out if he ever hurt her. Most of the time Devil was a laid-back president, and he didn't get involved with other people's troubles. With Ripper, Devil made an exception. If Ripper fucked up, Devil would shoot him. If he made Judi cry, Devil would shoot him. Every possibility when it came to Ripper, Devil had threatened. So far, Ripper was still alive.

"Take care of her," Judi said, snatching her soda from the counter as she passed him.

Spider stood behind the counter. "You want a drink?"

"No. I've got stuff to do."

Moving away from the bar he walked into the kitchen to find Dick and Amy fucking on one of the counters. Brianna wasn't in sight.

"You better clean up after you."

"Fuck off," Dick said.

Amy moaned, pulling Dick inside her. "Harder."

Shaking his head, he made his way up to his bedroom. He stopped outside of Brianna's room, tempted to walk inside the room. Reaching out he almost opened the door but stopped himself.

Pulling away, he made his way to his own room. Opening the door, he stopped as he caught sight of

Brianna sitting on the bed. Her hands were locked together in her lap. She looked at him without saying a word.

"What are you doing in here?" he asked.

"I wanted to talk to you." She tucked some of her red hair behind her ear. Did she have any idea how damn hot she looked?

He closed his bedroom door, leaning against it. Folding his arms over his chest, he stared at her, waiting. When she didn't speak or show signs of speaking, he did. "What did you want to talk to me about?"

"Your offer? Does it still stand?"

"You want to become my old lady?" She had another couple of days to decide. He wasn't going to rush her even though he wanted her with a desperation that shocked him. No woman had ever left him feeling like this. He needed to remind himself constantly that she wasn't like other women. She'd been used, and from the way she behaved, she rarely used anyone else.

"I don't want to become available to the other men."

It wasn't exactly the best answer he wanted. She'd rather be with him than anyone else. He was the lesser of two evils.

"This is not a decision to be made lightly, Brianna. I'm not going to let you go once I've got you." He wanted her to know right from the start that he had every intention of keeping her.

"There's nowhere else for me to go. I've got no family or friends. This is the only place I've got. You promised to be patient with me."

"I'm not going to wait around forever," he said, letting her know from the start he wanted more.

"I know. You'll give me time. I need time, and I promise I won't make you wait too long."

He nodded. "You can stay here tonight or you can have a final day in your room."

She glanced around the room. "Can I stay here?"

****

"Sure, you can stay here. I'm not going to kick you out of my room."

Brianna breathed out a sigh of relief. She'd really thought he might play a trick on her and have her out of his room where she'd have to start begging other brothers for a chance to be with them. Death made her feel something, and she'd not really felt anything but fear in a long time.

She still couldn't get the feel of his lips on hers out of her head. No matter how much she cleaned or cooked, the feel of his lips on hers along with his hands, stayed firmly in her mind. It was like her mind refused to forget something so amazing.

Reaching behind her she grabbed the clean pair of sweats she'd taken from her room. She felt awkward. What was she supposed to do now?

"You can use the bathroom first. It's through there." Death moved across his room. There wasn't a bathroom for her, and she needed to use the one the club whores were given to wash. She nodded, holding her bundle of clothes against her chest.

"Thank you, Death, I appreciate it." She stopped next to him. Brianna wanted to give him something. Staring at him, she watched him nod his head. This had to be one of the strangest moments of her life. Death was much older than she was, but she didn't care about his age.

He wasn't a good looking man in the fashionable way. There was something dark, terrifying about him. Whenever he looked at her, she knew he was waiting for her to do something. She'd never been watched or observed so closely before.

There were lines on either side of his eyes showing the maturity of his age. Where Pussy teased and tormented, she saw Death was serious all the time. He rarely let down his guard. The whole time she'd known him, apart from when she saw him getting a blow job, she'd never seen him with another woman.

The simple memory of seeing the blonde taking his cock twisted her gut. She was jealous of a woman she didn't know. Death wasn't hers.

He could be.

Death could be yours if you let him.

Give in, Brianna.

Judi's words from earlier came back to haunt her. She was giving her old master more power than he deserved. At twenty years old she'd not lived life or even known what she was missing out on. She didn't want to get to an age in life where she had nothing but constant regrets. That would be no life at all.

She stared at Death's lips remembering how amazing they felt on hers.

He's not like the others. This is what you want.

He'd not thrown her to the bed and fucked her. Death was going to give her time.

Stepping closer to him, she held her bundle of clothes in one hand while staring at him.

Do it.

Reaching out with her free hand, she ran her fingers up the front of his leather cut. He was strong, muscular. There was no doubt in her mind that Death could handle himself. She didn't know his real name, and if she was honest with herself, she didn't care. The last two years had taught her there was a hell of a lot more to people than their goddamn name.

She went on her toes while wrapping her arms

around his neck. Pressing her lips to his, she was surprised when he didn't respond at first. Brianna pulled back to look into his eyes. He stared right back without even blinking.

Mean it.

Licking her lips, she returned to kissing him, sliding her tongue along his lips. The passion she'd kept buried for so long, she released for him to feel. Regardless of what she tried to show everyone, she wasn't dead inside, far from it.

Passion, desire, need, want, hope—it was all in there waiting to be thrust out on the one man she wanted.

Dropping the clothes she held, she wrapped her arms around his neck, pressing her whole body against him. She craved the close contact with him.

The hard ridge of his cock pressed against her abdomen, letting her know exactly what he wanted from her. She wouldn't be ready tonight, but as she deepened the kiss something awakened inside her.

He didn't take advantage, giving her time to adjust to him.

When she would have continued, he grabbed her arms and held her away from him.

"Go and shower."

"But—"

"No, not tonight. I'm not going to do this with you." He cupped her cheek, dropping a kiss to her lips before finally stepping back.

She watched him turn and walk away.

Confusion hit her all at once. Why didn't he want to kiss her back?

He promised you time. Stop moaning about it and go shower.

Brianna closed the shower door. She saw the lock but didn't bother to use it. Dropping the clothes on the toilet seat, she stripped off and turned the shower on. She waited for the water to heat before climbing into the stall.

Licking her lips, she lifted her head up to the spray of water. Her heart was racing as she touched her lips once again. What was it about Death that had her body going crazy?

She glided a hand down, feeling the sensitiveness of her breasts. Going further down, she ran her fingers over her quivering stomach until she touched herself. Sliding a finger through her slit she was shocked by the wetness she discovered. The heat wasn't from the water but her own body.

Pressing a finger to her cunt, she slid a digit inside, biting down on her lip as the sudden onslaught of pleasure took her by surprise. Unable to stop herself, she pressed a thumb to her clit, groaning out.

"Brianna, are you okay?"

She didn't answer the question, sure that she was hearing things. Drawing her fingers up from her pussy, she began to work her clit.

"What the fuck?" Death said.

Gasping, she turned pressing her back against the shower. The doors were steamy, but she could make out his outline. What the hell had just happened? She tried to cover up her body as Death opened the stall.

"What are you doing?" she asked.

"I heard you groan. I didn't know what caused it."

"Nothing." She crossed her legs, desperate for some release. It was insane to think she'd never felt like this before.

Death didn't walk away. He stepped into the shower even though he was wearing some boxer briefs. He'd obviously gotten undressed while she was in the shower.

"You're getting wet," she said, daring to chance a look at him. In one quick movement, he closed the door, locking them both into the shower.

He stared down at her. The heat in his gaze made her shiver. Death didn't say anything as he grabbed her hands and slowly drew them away from her body, leaving her exposed to his gaze.

She didn't fight him.

The arousal coursing through her was on the verge of pain. Nothing felt like her own. She was used to not feeling or caring. This was new for her, and she knew it was all because of him that she was feeling this way.

With her hands by her side, she jerked as his fingers glided across her stomach. He didn't go down but worked his way up her body to cup her breasts. His thumb stroked across her nipple.

She released a moan, arching up against his hands.

No words were spoken. He played with her tits bringing her more pleasure. When she thought she was on the point of release, he stopped, sliding his hands down her stomach.

Each second that passed with his light touches only served to arouse her more. Brianna couldn't look away from him. She was hypnotized by the way he touched her. The gentle touches were not enough, but she saw he was holding back. Death was in complete control of his actions. She couldn't stop him, didn't want to stop him.

His fingers slid through her pubic hair. Death teased the strands of her hair moving down to finger her slit. One finger went between the lips of her pussy, opening her up. He stroked her clit as he moved down to touch her pussy. With only his one finger, he pressed inside her, and Brianna couldn't hold on anymore.

She gripped his arms as her legs almost gave out. Death moved her back until she pressed against the tiles that had warmed up from the heat of the shower. He kept her on her feet between the wall and his hard body. She'd closed her eyes for a split second, and when she opened them she saw he was close.

There was no fear, no pain, only pleasure and anticipation. She was in his arms, and there was nowhere else she wanted to go.

He added a second finger inside her, thrusting the two digits high inside her.

"Do you want more?" he asked.

It was the first time he'd spoken since joining her in the shower. Brianna simply nodded.

Yes, she wanted more. Whatever was happening to her body needed a hell of a lot more of what he could give her.

Death pressed his thumb against her clit, moving it back and forth. With his fingers inside her and his thumb on her nub, a mass of sensation exploded inside her. He kept her locked in place as he played with her body. She loved every second.

"You need release next time, Brianna, you come to me. I don't share what's mine and that includes your hand. I'll give you everything you need. I'll never force you. You want me to fuck you, ask, and I'll fuck you. I'll wipe every single fucking memory out of your mind of what that bastard did to you. When you're in my bed you'll scream in pleasure, not in pain. I will give you everything you've ever wanted."

She stared into his eyes as he spoke, knowing he said nothing but the truth. This was what she wanted. When she'd been alone at night after she'd been used, she would think about a man who'd want only her. She'd wished for a man who wouldn't share her, who'd be possessive, and who wouldn't hurt her.

Could Death be the very man she'd been hoping for all along?

Chapter Six

Brianna gripped his shoulders. Death watched her reactions, making sure she was with him the whole way. The water fell down around them getting his boxers wet, and he didn't care. Hearing her groan, he'd thought she'd hurt herself. He'd called her name several times trying to get her attention. Each time had been a failure. She wasn't answering him. He'd become worried. When he opened the door, the last thing he expected to see was Brianna playing with herself. The wonder he'd witnessed on her face would stay with him forever.

He released her pussy and took her lips in another searing kiss. When he went to touch her again he was stopped by her tugging on his briefs.

Within seconds he stood within the shower butt ass naked, like she was.

She reached out, running her fingers along the ink displayed on his abdomen. He didn't reach out to touch her. Death placed his hands on either side of her head against the wall, giving her free rein to touch his body. He was hers for the taking.

Staring down into her green eyes, he saw her gaze was on his body. He had the Chaos Bleeds symbol decorating his left hip. His body was a canvas for tribal tattoos, and whatever took his fancy. Death liked to get inked. When her hands moved from his abdomen to grip his cock, he let out a hiss.

"You don't have to do that." He covered her hand with his, intending to stop her.

"I want to. I want to give you pleasure." She gripped his cock a little harder.

Cupping her cheek, he slid his thumb across, touching her. "Only if you want to."

"I do."

He glided his hand down her body, touching her soft skin. She was so beautiful. From the moment he first saw her when they pulled her out of the strip club, he'd felt like he'd been punched in the gut. Her beauty was all natural. Nothing about her body was fake. Her tits were large, full, and spilled over his hand when he cupped them. She had nice wide hips, a rounded stomach, and an ass he could grip. The clothes she wore were in a larger size. He knew she was between a size sixteen to eighteen. Death couldn't be more accurate as he'd never paid much attention to the tag within the clothes he bought for her.

Yes, he'd been a fucking sucker and started to buy her clothes. Feeling like a pussy for buying feminine clothes, he'd kept them locked up within his closet. No one knew about them, and that was the way he liked it. Whatever took his fancy, he bought. There was a deep green summer dress in there to match her eyes.

Sucker.

He cupped her pussy within his palm. "If you're going to play then so am I." Pressing two fingers inside her cunt, he groaned as she started to work his cock. Her hand went from the base of his cock up to the tip. Brianna pulled his foreskin back, sliding a finger over the tiny slit at the top.

She didn't look away from him and neither did he with her.

Death intended for her to know at every turn the person she was with.

"Your hand feels so good, Brianna," he said.

With his fingers well lubricated from her cunt, he drew them up her slit to touch her clit. Her nub was swollen, and he slowly stroked her. He watched her eyes dilate, and her cheeks got flushed as he stroked her clit.

It was hard to concentrate with her hands on his

cock, but he did it. Pressing his advantage, he moved his fingers down to her cunt. He took his time teasing her clit before going back to her pussy. Death kept his other hand beside her head.

Neither of them looked away. Something passed between them. He didn't know what, but he wasn't about to stop to analyze it.

She used her other hand to cup his balls as she worked his cock.

"I want you to come on my fingers, Brianna. I'm going to watch as you come apart in my arms. I'll be here to hold you like always."

Keeping his fingers inside her, he caressed her clit with his thumb, watching her start to pant. Her chest heaved with each deep inhalation. The walls of her pussy tightened around his fingers. Leaning down, he claimed her lips, sliding his tongue inside her.

She didn't stop playing with his cock. The pleasure built inside him. His cock was so hard it was on the verge of pain. Death didn't stop her. He wasn't ready to stop her.

Nipping at her lips, Death plunged his fingers in as he pressed his thumb hard against her clit. Brianna cried out, breaking from the kiss as she came. She screamed out her release and worked her hand faster over his cock. Death dropped his head to the curve of her neck as his own release exploded out of him. He watched the white strands of his cum shoot onto her stomach. With the way he was standing, he stopped any water from washing his cum away. He liked seeing his seed on her body.

Death hoped soon he'd be climaxing inside her tight cunt and watching his seed slide from the lips of her pussy. He'd never taken a woman without a rubber, but with Brianna he was going to make an exception. She was going to be filled with his cum, and he'd be more than happy to keep on doing it.

They were both panting, and he removed his fingers from her tight heat. He pulled away and watched as the water washed down her body. His gaze was caught by the fine hairs of her pussy, which were a lighter red than the hair on her head. He'd not taken the time to actually look at the hairs of her pussy.

He wanted to taste her but knew that would come in time.

Taking a kiss, he plunged his tongue inside her mouth then withdrew.

"Thank you."

Death moved her away from the wall, and picked up the soap. Without saying a word, he lathered his hands and started to clean her body. She didn't fight him or tell him to stop.

When she was cleaned, he quickly washed his own body. He'd been outside, waiting for her to finish. That one groan had smashed all of his good intentions to smithereens.

Finished with his own body, he grabbed the soap, using it on her head first. He was surprised when she didn't try to take over. Brianna let him clean her, washing the shampoo from her hair before going onto the conditioner. She moved out of his way as he worked the soap into his own hair.

He turned off the shower, opened the door, and climbed out. Death gave Brianna a towel watching as she covered herself up in the grey towel. Her body was amazing. Death couldn't wait to have more time to explore what now belonged to him.

She climbed out of the stall, and stood off to the side.

Death leaned down, wringing out his clothes.

"I don't know what came over me," she said.

He glanced at her over his shoulder.

"One moment I didn't know what was happening, the next moment, I wanted you naked."

Death smiled. "You're attracted to me, Brianna." He was downright smitten with her. "When we're together I want you to understand that you can talk to me. Don't be afraid of me."

He didn't want her to be scared. Throughout his life he'd scared both men and women. Scaring men didn't bother him, but he didn't like the thought of women being scared of him, especially this woman.

"I'm not afraid of you."

Standing back up, he threw the clothes into the trash. His jacket he draped over the radiator by the toilet. She held the towel against her chest tight. Her knuckles were white with how tight she held it.

"Are you sure about that?" he asked, staring at her hands.

She glanced down at her hands then back up at him. "I've never done anything like this. I mean, I've had sex. I've had a lot of sex."

"It's not sex that you've wanted." He stared at her. Death was a good foot taller than she was. He held a towel wrapped around his waist.

Brianna's hair was wet from the shower. She looked so tempting standing by the door waiting for him. "No, I didn't want it," she said, shaking her head.

He had to remind himself of what he said.

"With me you'll only ever do what you want. I meant what I said in the shower. You want an orgasm, come to me. Until you're ready, you'll start everything."

"What do you mean?" she asked.

"I get that you've probably done everything. You've fucked for survival, sucked cock, probably even taken it up the ass to survive." The way her cheeks heated, he got his answer. "What I'm saying to you is forget all of it. It happened, and I'm not going to pretend it didn't. Your first sexual experience was about being used. You don't know what it's like to want someone. What I mean is, if you want me to touch you, I won't until you ask me to. You'll tell me every single step of the way what you want me to do to you." If her cheeks got any redder she'd be on fucking fire. He took a step closer to her. "You want me to touch your pussy, tell me. You want to suck my cock, tell me. You want me to take you out some place, tell me." He stopped when he was right in front of her. "If you want me to bend you over the bed and fuck you like you've never been fucked before, tell me. Until you're ready, you control everything that happens to you."

"If I don't want any of that?"

Death smiled. The passion inside her glowed brighter than ever before, and it was so damn easy to see.

"You'll want it, Brianna." He leaned in close. "I know exactly how to make sure you do want it without taking anything from you." Again, he dropped a kiss to her lips, before making his way into his bedroom.

He dropped the towel before climbing into bed.

"You're not going to put any clothes on?" she asked.

"No, you don't have to either. I won't touch you, Brianna. I'm not some little schoolboy who doesn't understand what no means." He placed the blanket over his crotch, looking back at her. She seemed so unsure of herself. "I'm not going to kick you out of my room or my bed if you wear a shirt. Damn, wear a coat, hat, gloves, and scarf if it'll make you feel comfortable."

She quickly wriggled into a shirt, pulling on a pair of shorts to go underneath. It was such a shame for her to go clothed. In time he'd have her naked and waiting for him.

Brianna moved to the bed. He watched her hands open and close, staring down at the blanket with him inside it.

Come on, baby, get inside.

He didn't say a word aloud, waiting for her to climb into bed.

Grabbing the remote from his drawer, he pointed it at the television and started to flick through the channels. He wasn't going to rush her.

****

Get in the bed.

Death paid her no attention as Brianna stared at the bed. He would be the first man she'd ever shared a bed with. She cut off her other thoughts as Master tried to invade her mind. *He* was the last person she was going to think of. Death flicked through channels giving her space.

He didn't look in her direction.

Feeling like a total idiot, she lifted the covers and climbed into bed. Turning onto her side, she stayed as far away from him as possible.

Seriously? You've had his cock in your hand. You've given him an orgasm and you're going to lie there?

"Remember what I said, Brianna?"

She glanced over her shoulder to see him still looking at the television screen.

"The only way something is going to happen between us is if you initiate it. You've got nothing to be afraid of."

Brianna nodded then turned so that she faced the screen. Slowly, she began to move her pillow to get more comfortable. When she was in a better position she sat and watched the movie.

"I'll be back in a minute," Death said, climbing out of bed. She watched him pull on a pair of sweats before leaving the room. Brianna pressed a hand to her chest. His ass was nice and firm. She imagined gripping the flesh and pulling him deeper inside her as she got closer to orgasm.

Get your thoughts out of the gutter.

She watched the horror movie playing on the screen. It was about a clown terrorizing a group of children. Clowns didn't scare her.

Death returned minutes later with his arms full with food. He dropped the bags of chips, candy, and chocolate onto the bed.

"Here, I got this for you." He handed her a soda then placed his on the drawer beside his bed. She held the cold can in her hands. Out of the corner of her eye she watched him drop his pants before getting back into bed.

"Why don't you keep your pants on?" she asked.

"I can't sleep with them on."

He opened a bag of cheesy flavored chips, offering some up to her. She took some of the chips, drinking soda as she watched the movie. When he opened the candy along with the chocolate, she took some of what he offered.

She moaned around the caramel covered chocolate at the same time Death did. Brianna smiled at him, and he smiled back at her.

It was … nice. There were no expectations of her or demand that she do anything. They were simply sharing treats while also watching a movie together. Any tension she had left began to fade away with the movie.

"I like seeing you smile," Death said.

She turned her head to look at him to see him

staring back at her. Brianna didn't even realize she was smiling.

"I'm not a freak or anything. I wasn't smiling at the film."

He began to laugh. "What were you smiling at?"

"This, I've not been this relaxed in a long time. I'm enjoying myself."

"Well, you're the cheapest woman I know to get to enjoy herself. Most of them I know demand jewelry, fine wine, dinner, good sex."

She could tell he was teasing. The club whores didn't need anything other than sex. "Thank you for this."

"You don't need to thank me." He offered her some more cheesy chips. "Regardless of what people think, I actually like doing boring shit, too."

Brianna stared down at the chip in her hand before popping it into her mouth. "You watched a movie with any of the other women?"

Death stared at her. "Feeling a little jealous there?"

"No." The lie came out a lot easier than she thought possible.

He chuckled. "The sweet-butts or club whores don't stick around to watch a movie. They're interested in one thing and that's getting cock. No, I've never watched a movie with anyone else." He frowned. "Actually, I have. I watched them with Ashley and Pussy, but that doesn't count."

"I've heard about Ashley. She's a woman you all lost to Gonzalez?"

"Yeah, her death hit us all hard. We couldn't protect her. There was no way to warn her of what was happening." He stared ahead of him without seeing anything. She knew what that was like, remembering family and friends from the past.

"She sounded like a great woman."

"Ashley, she was different. Yeah, she liked to fuck like most of the club whores, but she was loyal with it. She didn't try for the men who were already taken. June is a little like her, only not as loyal. Ashley, she meant something to the club. She put other's needs before her own."

"You sound a little in love with her," Brianna said, feeling torn by his obvious feelings for the other woman.

Death burst out laughing. "No, I didn't love Ashley. I cared about her like a friend, not like a lover. Make no mistake, I fucked her. Most of the men here did, but it wasn't that kind of love. You'd have liked her. She had a rough start in life. It shouldn't have ended for her like it did." He shrugged. "There's not a lot to do to change what happened. We're all different now."

She took some candy, popping it into her mouth. Ashley had meant so much to all of them. Even Lexie and the other old ladies were fond of her.

"You're the first woman I've done this with in my room. When I watched a movie with Ashley and Pussy, we were down in the main room. This, this is much better." He took a drink of soda, leaning back. "I like that you're jealous, but you don't need to be. I'm not going to be fucking any other woman but you."

"You had a sweet-butt sucking your dick the other day." She recalled the blonde he'd had between his legs, sucking his length. The jealousy had surprised her at seeing him take pleasure in another woman.

Death chuckled. "It's good to know I finally got your attention."

"What?"

"It was a hard day. I wanted you, but I couldn't

have you. You showed no signs of wanting me. I needed some release, and she was there. Believe me, Brianna, it wasn't her that I wanted. It was you."

"Are you going to go with other women?" She knew he said he wouldn't, but men as well as women, lied to get what they wanted.

"No. I told you I'm not interested in other women. You're the only one that I want."

She was silent as the movie came to an end. Finishing off her soda, she climbed out of bed going to the bathroom. There was an extra toothbrush waiting in the holder. She gave it a wash before brushing her teeth. Death joined her, naked, as she brushed her teeth.

It was hard for her to not stare at him. He was so much larger than she was that he made her feel small in comparison to him. Death moved around her, not pushing her out of the way as he brushed his own teeth. Brianna gave up the fight of trying not to watch him. He stared back at her in the mirror as she watched him.

When she finished, she cleaned her brush and walked back into the room. The snacks had been moved off the bed. She was surprised to see the bed freshly made without a crumb in sight.

Climbing into the warm bed, she faced the bathroom, watching him walk out. Heat filled her cheeks as she saw the evidence of his arousal. He was rock hard again.

Heat spilled between her thighs at the sight of him.

The bed dipped, and the light went out. She rested on her side of the bed as he settled down.

For the longest time Brianna stared ahead of her in the darkness.

"You can relax. I don't bite."

She couldn't help but smile. Forcing herself to

relax was the hardest thing. The night wore on, and she found herself closing her eyes.

In no time at all, she fell asleep.

Chapter Seven

Death woke first to Brianna in his arms. She was fast asleep curled up against him. Her hands lay underneath her head, and she was looking up at him. She looked so peaceful that for several minutes he didn't move. One of his arms was underneath a pillow and the other lay over her body.

When she had fallen asleep last night, he had pulled her into his arms. He liked having her in his bed, close to him. There was no worry of him waking up to find that she'd left the clubhouse completely.

She's all yours.

He needed to talk with Devil and the rest of the club. Also, his bladder was begging for attention. He pulled his arm out from under her head first, the eased out of bed. At first, he stopped to wait for her to get comfortable. When he was sure she was going to continue sleeping, he left the room, going to the bathroom. He went to the toilet, washed his hands, brushed his teeth, then gathered his clothes, getting dressed.

Death watched her as he dressed. She looked totally different without the stress of the day plaguing her.

He went to his closet pulling out a pair of jeans and a green shirt he'd bought especially for her. Death put the underwear on top before leaving the room. Making his way out of the room, he saw the rest of the clubhouse was only just waking up. It was cold, and the first thing he did was put the heating on as he made his way into the kitchen.

"You look way too perky," Pussy said, sitting down at the table. He ran a hand over his face after opening the back door. Sasha's dog scrambled out of the door to go do her business.

"I'll start the coffee."

"It's a surprise Brianna isn't up. She usually takes care of the coffee, the heating, the dog, all of it." Pussy yawned, closing the door, and sitting at the table.

"She's in my bed," Death said, filling the coffee pot up.

"You finally got her in your bed?" Pussy asked.

"She was in my room last night when I got there."

"You're claiming her?"

"Yeah. She doesn't want to screw any of you ugly bastards, and I don't want her to."

Pussy gave him the finger, getting to his feet as his woman's dog started to scratch at the door. "Sasha's still in bed. She's coming down with the flu I think. It's the bad weather we're having. Her mom should be due home any day now. I still don't like her being near her mother."

"It was her stepfather's fault."

"If her bitch of a mother hadn't been high on drugs and booze, Sasha would still be able to see."

"You don't know that. Nothing could have stopped what happened."

Pussy shrugged.

"I thought you didn't mind her blindness." Death turned to look at his brother. Pussy was petting the dog in front of him.

"I don't. I love Sasha with all of my heart. I'd never let anything happen to her. I'd die for her, that's how much I fucking love her. Christmas, the tree, all of it, it makes me so fucking angry."

"Why?"

"She can't see any of it. Yeah, she can feel shit, know what's going on, but she can't see it. I leave my boots in the room and I don't tell her where they are she tumbles, bangs her head. God, I love her, and it's because I love her so damn much that I'm terrified. I hate what she can't have. I can't give her back her eyesight. I can't give her fuck all really."

When they'd put the tree up, he was sure he'd seen the sadness inside Pussy's eyes. This just confirmed it to Death.

"You've given her a hell of a lot, Pussy."

"Yeah? What?"

Death poured them both a hot cup of coffee, taking a seat beside his friend.

"Well, besides the obvious in a dog and stability, you've given her, you." Death took a sip of his coffee. "You've given her a family. All of us will take care of her. Yeah, Devil's not a big fan, but he won't let shit happen to her."

"I can't give her back the one thing she needs."

"She doesn't need it, Pussy. Sasha has got you. It's not your responsibility to give her everything. You love her regardless, right?"

"Of course I do. She means everything to me."

"Then what's the worry? Sasha doesn't need her eyesight. If you were to ask her if she could spend the rest of her life with you or get her eyesight, I know she'd pick you." The whole club knew she'd pick Pussy. She was completely in love with him. There was no room for doubt when it came to her feelings.

"Shit, I'm sorry, man. I shouldn't have unloaded on you like that."

Death shrugged. "I don't mind. Sasha's a great woman."

The dog barked like he was agreeing.

Pussy chuckled. "Come on. Let's go and wake her up. Thanks for the pep talk."

He walked out of the kitchen, taking his coffee

with him.

"That was a good talk you gave him," Mia said, entering the room.

"I'd not seen you wake up."

"Curse is being a lazy ass. It's my turn to fetch coffee. Anyone would think you're all bears with the way you stay camped out in bed." Mia walked over to the coffee pot, pouring out two mugs full. He watched her put plenty of sugar in one and none in the other. "I'm happy you're taking Brianna."

Death nodded. What else was he supposed to say? Out of all of the women Mia was the one he rarely spoke to. When all the shit kicked off with Gonzalez, he'd blamed Mia. If it wasn't for that fucker who attacked her, Curse would never have killed the bastard, and Gonzalez would never have entered their lives.

Lexie, Devil, and the kids entered, stopping him from having to talk to the woman. Mia took her coffee, leaving the room.

"I'm fine, Devil. Stop fussing," Lexie said, pressing the back of her hand to her face. "What is it?" Death asked.

"She doesn't like the smell of coffee. It's always the same with pregnancy. I'm getting the fucking snip after this one." Devil put Elizabeth to the table while Lexie dealt with their youngest son. Simon climbed up onto the table. In his hands was a video game. The sound was turned down, but there was no way anyone was getting that boy's attention away from the tiny device.

"Where's Brianna?" Lexie asked, opening cupboards.

"She's in bed. My bed," he said.

Both Lexie and Devil turned to look at him.

"You claiming her?" Devil asked.

"I'm claiming Tabitha," Simon said, shouting at

the top of his lungs. He looked over the top of his game to smile at his father.

"Lex!"

"Leave it, Devil. He's just a boy."

Simon was just a boy, but he certainly knew what he wanted.

"Tabitha's going to be all mine."

Devil shook his head, looking up to the ceiling. "Going to be the death of me."

Death heard the mutter from Devil.

Sipping at his coffee, Death watched the happy family working around the kitchen. "Yeah, I'm going to be claiming Brianna as my old lady."

"Are you sure she's ready for that?" Lexie asked.

"Doesn't have much of a choice. I'm going to give her time, but she's going to be mine."

Lexie and Devil shared a look.

"If that's what you want," Devil said. "I'm not going to step in the way."

"It's what I want. I'm taking her out today. I was going to ask what shopping you needed. The roads are not the best, and it's getting harder to ride on them. I'm taking the car so I can pick up any shopping you need."

"Oh, I've got a list." Lexie moved out of the room leaving Devil to tend to their breakfast.

Death watched as his president dumped cereal in a bowl for all of them. Simon didn't look down from his game. The little boy reached out, taking the spoon and started to eat his food.

Shaking his head, Death was still chuckling as Lexie walked back in the room carrying a long list. Behind him, he saw Brianna waiting. She was dressed in the jeans and shirt he'd left out for her.

"Hey," she said, smiling at him. "I, erm, I found these when I woke up."

His dick went from flaccid to hard in a second. "I left them for you." Aware of the gazes on them, Death walked out of the room, grabbing her arm as they walked out of the clubhouse. They were met by freezing cold air.

He cursed as she gasped at the sudden chill.

Neither of them was wearing coats. When they were in the truck, he turned the ignition over heating up the small vehicle.

"It's freezing. What's the rush?" she asked, rubbing at her arms.

The clothes he'd put out were not the best for this weather.

"I'm sorry. I just wanted us to have some alone time. Devil and Lexie are not alone time."

He pulled out of the clubhouse, handing over the list of shit Lexie wanted. "Here, have a look through this."

"Turkey, ham, beef, chicken, tomatoes," Brianna said, going silent as she looked over to him. "We're food shopping?"

"It would seem that way. We'll stop off at the diner in the town. It's a good place, and you'll love the food. Mia used to work there. Curse put an end to that."

"Pussy, Curse, Devil, Death, you've all got strange names. Is it your real name?"

Death chuckled. "No, not even close."

"What's your real name?"

"Benjamin. You use that name and I swear I'll torture you with orgasms," he said, shooting a wink her way.

She started to laugh along with him. He loved the sound of her laughing. Death wanted to keep her laughing.

"They're our road names. We've earned our names."

"Do I even want to know how Pussy earned his name?"

Death smiled. "There were a lot of women in Pussy's life. It took him a long time to get the name."

"How?"

"He eats pussy. Pussy loves pussy. It's how he got his name."

"Okay, I really didn't need to know that."

"You ever had you pussy eaten?"

"No."

He looked over at her. "When you're ready to remedy that little fact, I'll show you how damn good it can be to have your pussy licked and sucked."

Her cheeks were flushed once again. A quick glance down and he saw her nipples were budded against the shirt. Part of it could be down to how cold it was while another could be down to arousal. He was going to go with arousal more than the cold. The heating was on in the car.

"Okay, Curse?"

"He was fucking cursed. We went on a run, and whatever could go wrong with him, did. The man was fucking cursed. The name stuck." Death slowed down the car as they were entering town. This early in the morning kids would be crossing the road without looking, which always pissed him off.

"Butler?"

"Before the drink and drugs took over there was a time when Butler acted like that. He lived to serve. He was also in the army for a long time, served his country. When he got out, it fucked with his head. Since Devil ordered the club to be clean, Butler has started to look normal again."

"Should you be telling me all this?" she asked.

"Why?"

"Some kind of loyalty or code or something."

"You're my woman, Brianna. Your loyalty is to me and the club."

****

Brianna liked that. There was no way she'd ever do anything to put Chaos Bleeds in danger. She owed them her life. If they'd not come into the strip club when they had, she'd have been servicing men by the hour. She shuddered at the thought. Since the crew had entered her life, she'd changed. Waking up that morning surrounded by Death's scent, she'd felt happy, safe. It was nice to finally feel like herself again.

When she saw the clothes out waiting for her, she'd been touched. Had they belonged to someone else?

Death hadn't removed the tag from inside the jeans. They were brand new jeans. Had he brought them for her?

She didn't know, and right now she wasn't ready to have the answer to her own questions.

He pulled up in the parking lot in the town. She'd not seen much of Piston County, and with the snow, it was hazardous to be moving around. Brianna took the hand he offered, following him inside into the diner. He took the booth near the door.

"Here." Death passed her a menu, which she looked over while he ordered coffees.

Brianna picked what she wanted, holding the warm mug between her cold hands.

"We should have picked up our jackets."

"Tell me about it. I'm freezing my nuts off." Death held the cup, twirling the menu around for him to have a look. "You decided what you want?"

"Eggs benedict. My mom used to make them for me." Brianna smiled, recalling the love and affection that used to embrace her.

"I'm sorry you lost your family. Ending up with Ronald was the worst fucking thing for any woman."

She stared down at the coffee in her cup. Brianna hated coffee. The smell, the taste, but she couldn't bring herself to stop drinking it. Unlike most people she'd never acquired a taste for the bitter liquid. She preferred a sweet tea.

"What's going on in your head?" he asked.

"It's nothing."

"If you don't want the coffee I can order something else for you," he said.

"What makes you think I don't want the coffee?"

He leaned over the table. "You're looking down like shit is in your cup. You don't want it, let me know."

She opened her mouth then closed it, frowning.

"I can't change shit if you don't talk about it."

"I hate coffee." The words spilled from her lips, yet it was a struggle.

Death leaned back and smiled. "Why didn't you say so?"

Brianna shrugged. "It has been easier pretending." She'd pretended all the time with Master.

"You don't need to pretend with me." He signaled the waitress, grabbing her attention. "Hey, doll, could you change this to—" Death looked over at her.

"Sweet tea," Brianna said.

The cup was taken from her and replaced by a cup of sweet tea.

"See, I told you."

She took a sip, and it tasted like heaven.

"What about Snake's name?" Brianna asked, changing the subject. She liked having his attention focused on her. They were away from the clubhouse and all the distractions that came with it.

"He's fucking deadly, like a snake. The bastard

may not seem that tough, but one snap from him, you're fucking dead."

She knew it had to be true.

"Devil's name?"

"Worst of us all. You fuck up you answer to him. We've all sold our soul to the devil, but it's for a good cause. Devil is a lot of dangerous things, yet he's got morals. They're our code, and we stick to them. There was a time when we wouldn't stick in the same place. We moved around, caused shit wherever we went."

"What changed?"

"Simon. Devil heard a whore had given birth to his son and left him alone with her sister. This shit you can't say anywhere else."

"Simon's not Lexie's son?"

"No, he's not. There's no reason for him to ever find out either."

"I won't tell." Her respect for Lexie went up a hell of a lot. "What about your name?"

He sighed, looking toward her. "You don't want to know."

"Why?" She was curious about him. Brianna wasn't an idiot. She knew whatever his name meant was bad shit, maybe even the worst.

The waitress came over interrupting their meal. Brianna waited for Death to finish ordering their meals before asking him a question once again.

Death ran a hand down his face. "I've not been a good man, Brianna. Don't expect for my story to be all sunshine and roses. It's not. I've killed people, lots of people. I get the job done. This shit with Gonzalez, it was the first time I've ever had to hold back. I hated it. My name is Death because that is exactly what I bring, death."

She had to be a fucking idiot. Brianna knew his

name was bad, but she didn't care. Death hadn't hurt her. He'd given her nothing but pleasure and safety.

"Do you want to run from me now?"

Sipping at her sweet tea, she shook her head. "No, I don't."

"Why not?"

"You don't scare me." She sat back, staring at him.

He faced her fully, giving her his undivided attention. "I don't scare you?"

"No."

"Then what do I do to you?"

Brianna stared back at him. Her pulse raced, and her mouth went dry.

"You do a lot of things to me."

"Like what?" He reached over taking hold of her hand. His hand was larger and his fingers rougher as he stroked over the inside of her wrist. "What are you feeling now?"

"Nervous." It was the first word that came to mind. "Excited. For so long I've been caught up in a world of fear. When I'm around you I forget everything and I want to be me. I want to be normal without any fear or revulsion."

"You don't have to be afraid."

"Even though you bring death?" she asked, smiling.

"We both know I'll never hurt you."

She did know, which was strange to her. "I thought my life was over when I was sent to *him*. You make me want to live again."

He locked their fingers together. She crossed her legs as more warmth seeped from the lips of her pussy.

"Your pussy is wet."

Brianna opened her mouth to say something to

him when the waitress came toward them. Eggs benedict was placed in front of her while his pancakes with eggs and bacon was given to him. The waitress didn't add an extra smile. She simply put the plates down then left.

"Well, is your pussy wet for me?"

She glanced around the diner to see no one was paying any attention to them. A thrill worked through her at his words. Remembering what he said about making sure she wanted him, Brianna knew he was going to be successful. Even now, she wanted him. They were in a diner about to eat breakfast and all she could think about was his lips between her thighs. What would it be like to have him licking at her pussy?

He released her hands, and she picked up a fork. She cut into the egg, watching the yolk fall out over the plate. Taking a bite, she groaned at the taste. It really was a delicious meal.

"Yes," she said.

He chewed on his pancake, smiling at her. "You want me?"

"Yes."

Death arched a brow. "What are you going to do about it?"

She took another bite of her food. "I don't know."

"You better think of something, baby."

They ate the rest of the food in silence. The sexual tension mounted with every passing minute. Her nipples hardened as she thought about his lips on her body. She didn't ask him for anything, following him out to the truck. He drove out of town toward the supermarket. It had been so long since she'd done something as mundane as shopping. For several minutes she followed him around as he piled the trolley high. When she saw something she wanted, she asked Death's permission to add it. After the tenth item he told her to just put it in. When she went to argue, the scowl on his face stopped her.

She didn't want to put him in a bad mood.

His scowl didn't last for long. Death kept asking her to bend down to get cans from the bottom shelf or cartons. It took her a good fifteen minutes to realize he was doing it on purpose to check out her ass. She still did it. Only she got a thrill every time she bent down knowing his gaze was on her ass.

"Did you buy these clothes for me?" she asked, handing him a bottle of chocolate sauce.

Death stared at her, taking the sauce from her hands. "I bought them."

"Did you buy them for me or for someone else?" She stopped him from moving with a hand on the trolley keeping him in place.

He released a sigh. "Are you going to let it go?"

She shook her head. "No."

"I bought them for you."

"Why?"

Neither of them backed down. Death didn't avert his gaze. He just kept staring at her. "Because I saw them and knew you'd look fucking amazing in them."

"Did you always know I was going to say yes?" she asked. Was she really a sure thing?

"No, I didn't have a fucking clue. I was going to stay away from you. You're too damn young for me anyway."

"Why didn't you?"

"I decided I didn't give a damn. You came to me, Brianna. I merely offered you a place in my life. It was half your decision. If you don't want to be there, tell me. I'll still provide for you, but it'll get you out of the club."

She didn't want to be away from him. The moment she moved out of the club the club whores would be at him. The very thought of June, Amy, and the others pawing at him filled her with disgust. No, she didn't want to be out of his life.

"I'm happy with being part of the club life," she said. "I've made my decision. I'm not going to back out of it." Not only was she going to be part of his life, she wanted to be in his bed, giving him exactly what he needed, pleasure.

"Good. Be prepared for more clothes. I've got plenty for you, and yes, I bought them with you in mind."

Tucking some hair behind her ear, Brianna got a thrill at his sweet side. She doubted many women saw this side of Death.

This was what she wanted to see all the time. Brianna knew in that moment she'd do whatever it took to keep him in her life.

****

Snake stood outside the library freezing his balls off while Judi was inside grabbing a book. Ripper had an errand to run for Devil, which left him to run her to the library. He was sure she had more than enough books, but she was always looking for another one. Wrapping his leather jacket around him, Snake glared at the snow, wishing he could melt it away with his gaze alone.

Death and Brianna were together, which worked well for the club. Snake never should underestimate his president. Devil knew what everyone was thinking and feeling before even they did. It was completely insane, yet there was no other way to describe it.

"Come on, Judi." If he didn't get some warmth soon he was going to end up with frostbite on his dick.

Walk into the library.

He would have done if he'd not seen the tempting raven haired siren who'd been irritating him the past couple of days. She walked down the street staring into shop windows. Her hair was down, blowing around her. The coat she wore covered her body, but the nurse's uniform she'd been in had put every curve on display. She was fucking beautiful. He'd be more than happy to show her a good time. Snake wouldn't even need a bed to show her how fucking good he could be.

Out of all the women she could be friends with, Lydia was the last person he wanted her to know. He wasn't going to get into her pants with Lydia around.

Jessica came to a stop when she clocked him.

"Are you following me?" he asked, giving her a grin.

She stood glaring at him. "You'd like that, wouldn't you?"

"What can I say? I've got that effect on women."

"Ugh, what did she ever see in you? You're disgusting." She shook her head.

This was not the warmest of receptions he'd ever been given from a woman. He wasn't going to give up.

"You're going to take her opinion of me instead of making one of your own?" He took a step closer.

"Did you or did you not fuck my friend and leave her? Didn't even call?"

"When I fucked Lydia I never said anything about extra time. We were a one-time deal."

"Yet you fucked around the back of the diner, then went back with her to her place and fucked throughout the night."

She said all of that without taking a breath.

"Don't you women ever not talk about the men you've slept with?"

"What? We can't be like guys talking about our latest conquests?" She averted her gaze to across the street. He heard her release a frustrated sigh. "Why the hell am I still talking to you?"

Jessica started to walk past him. He caught her arm trying to get her to stay. It was sick and stupid, but even with her throwing insults at him, he'd never felt so alive. "Get to know me."

"You've got to be joking."

"One date. That's all I'm asking, one date."

She stopped to glare at him. "Will you stop it? I'm not going on a date with you. Haven't you ever heard about loyalty?"

"What about all is fair in love and war?"

"We're not at war, and we're certainly not in love." She tried to pull away, but he pulled her closer.

"One date. Give me one date and I promise you I'll back away."

Jessica stared at him. "One date but you've got to call Lydia and officially break it off. She's still waiting for you."

Woman's fucking crazy.

"Fine." One date with Jessica, he'd do anything she said. "I get to pick what we do."

"Okay." She glanced down at his hand on her arm. "Going to let me go?"

He released her. At the same time Judi came out of the library carrying a bag full of books.

Snake grabbed the sack off her.

"I can carry those," Judi said, placing a hand over her stomach.

"You're pregnant."

"Is this your girlfriend?" Jessica asked, looking angry.

Judi frowned. "Huh?"

"I can't believe you. Arranging dates and screwing women and you've already knocked up one woman." Jessica's voice rose with each word she spat out at him. He saw the anger in her eyes but also the hurt.

He didn't like how seeing the hurt in her eyes affected him.

"Whoa, lady. I'm not his woman. I'm married to one of his brothers, Ripper," Judi said, holding her hands up. "He brought me along to the library after drawing the short straw." He went to argue, but she turned to look at him. "Yeah, you did draw the short straw. Ripper already told me how you all deal with chores like this." She returned her attention back to Jessica. "He's perfectly free. Believe me I wouldn't be dating him. It's nice to meet you." Judi offered her a hand.

"Yeah, it's nice meeting you. I'm ever so sorry."

Snake was going to enjoy chasing after this woman.

Chapter Eight

Death watched Brianna interacting with all of the other old ladies as she helped to unpack all of their purchases from the supermarket. The tree was fully decorated with the kids' attempts at decorations. The star on the top was made by Simon with lots of help from the brothers. Death was shocked by how much fun everyone was actually having from being part of the fun.

For the first time in the Chaos Bleeds clubhouse the scent of mince pies wafted through the house filling him with joy. The smells were amazing, as were the carols Lexie had put on for them all to listen to. He even saw Dick was having fun in the corner singing along with Sasha and Pussy.

"She's a good one," Lexie said, passing him.

"What?"

"You break down those walls she's so damn determined to keep up and you've got a keeper." Lexie carried a tray of baked mince pies as she went. He watched her walk away handing out her bounty.

Entering the kitchen, he saw Judi rolling out pastry while Mia was filling the cups with mincemeat. The happiness within the whole club was strange. For so long they'd all be tense with the comings and goings of Gonzalez. This new feeling of peace seemed short lived. He turned to see Brianna coming from the store room Lexie had demanded they have. There were far too many men to feed to just leave it blank. Devil had once said it was going to be a store for guns, after which Lexie refused to have sex with him. It was funny to watch. Devil had had every intention of filling the room with food. His president just liked to tease Lexie until she was fuming.

Brianna gave him a big smile, moving toward

him. When she was in front of him he saw her hands open and close into fists as if she was unsure of what to do next.

"It's okay, baby."

He waited and was rewarded as she ran her hands up his chest to circle his neck.

"I really enjoyed today."

His cock hardened at how close she was. "I'm pleased." Resting his hands on her waist, he waited for to take the next step. Again, he didn't need to wait long as she went to her toes and pressed a tame kiss to his lips.

The smallest kiss from her lips and it was enough to drive him crazy. He wanted more, needed more.

Groaning, he pulled away, removing his hands as she frowned at him.

"You call that a kiss? My grandmother gave strange men better welcomes," Snake said, walking into the room.

The disappointment in her eyes was clear to see.

"Shut the fuck up, Snake, before I put you into an early grave."

"You can't put him in an early grave," Judi said, wiping her hands on a towel. "He's got a hot date with a hot nurse."

"Jessica?" Death asked, looking between the two.

"The one and only," Snake said. "We'll see how long she can refuse my rustic charms."

Lexie and Devil were walking into the kitchen as Snake said that last part. Both of them started laughing.

"What?" Snake asked, glaring at everyone. They were all laughing at him.

"Rustic? You're plain damn rust. You've not got a single romantic bone in your body. It's all rust." Devil slapped him on the back.

"I wouldn't start commenting, Devil. You could

still learn a thing or two." Lexie raised a brow at her husband.

"Do you want to get out of here?" Death asked, wanting out of the way when the claws came out.

"Yes, there's somewhere I want to go." Brianna took his hand, surprising him further as she made her way up to the backstairs toward his bedroom. Once they were inside their room she closed the door, leaning heavily against it. She didn't say anything as she looked at him.

"Why did you bring me here?" he asked, leaving everything to her.

"Because I couldn't get the memory of your tongue out of my head. I remember what you said last night. Whatever I want you'll give me." She took a visible deep breath and took a step toward him. "I want to give you something."

"What?" His cock was threatening to explode out of his pants. This was all on her. Death wasn't going to push her.

"I want to suck your cock."

Okay, out of everything he thought she could have said that was the last thing he anticipated. His cock didn't protest. In fact, he was happy to get naked and let her have her wicked way with him.

"Why?"

She took a step toward him. Her hands rested on his abdomen, and it took every ounce of control not to force her hands further down. Instead, he stood before her without touching, waiting. Would he always be waiting for her?

This is what you want, dickhead.

"I don't want you going anywhere else for your pleasure. When I saw that sweet-butt sucking you off, I got angry and hurt. I didn't like it. If I'm to come to you for pleasure then I want you to come to me."

He touched her cheek, stroking the delicate flesh. "Baby, I got her to suck my dick so I could look at you. She may have had her mouth around me, but I was only thinking about you."

"I don't care." She pushed him back until the edge of the bed forced him to sit down on the top.

"You're going to need me to get my pants off before you can suck me."

"What's the rush?" She tugged off her shirt showing the plain black lace bra he'd given her. This was a side to Brianna he never expected to see so early on. He liked it and didn't want it to stop.

Once again she stood before him clenching and unclenching her hands. He wasn't going to do anything to encourage her actions. This was going to be all her.

"There's no rush. I'm here for you to do whatever you want." Every other woman he'd have them on the bed and fucking them by now. This was different. This was Brianna, and he wanted her to enjoy this time as much as he did.

"You're right." She opened and closed her hand then bent down to grab his hands. This had to be one of the strangest things in his life. Not once had he let a woman take the lead in the bedroom. She pressed his hand to her naked stomach.

He kept his hand still and stared at her, waiting.

"I'm not going to do anything, baby. This is you all the way."

"I want you to touch me," she said.

"Where?"

"I want you to touch my breasts."

"Tits, baby. Call them what they are, and in this room, they're tits. There's no room for anything else. They're tits. My tits."

"Please, Death, touch my tits."

The arousal intensified. Running his fingers up her stomach, he kept his gaze on hers, refusing to back down. This was what they both wanted, craved. He was going to give her exactly what she asked for and not anything else.

Death crept up, cupping her breasts that were covered by the lace. She gave a groan of frustration.

"What?" he asked.

"More, I need more."

"Then take your bra off. Remember, Brianna, you control all of this. Not me. This is all you."

She groaned, but he watched as she removed her bra. Her large tits spilled out of the cups, and she flung the bra to the side. The sight of her naked flesh was more than enough to drive him to distraction.

It took all of his control not to grip his cock and tug her to the bed.

Patience.

He'd never been a man known for his patience, taking what he wanted when he wanted it.

She's different.

Brianna was different. He didn't need to rush to be with her. She didn't know how turned on he already was and they'd only been together a few short days. He'd been hooked from that first kiss.

Cupping her naked tits, he ran his thumb along the tip. "Like this, baby. You want me to touch you like this."

"Yes." She looked down at where he touched her then to his gaze. "I want more."

"What do you want?" He pinched her nipples drawing a little bite of pain only stopping when she had enough.

"I want you. I want everything you can give me,"

she said, moaning.

"You want my mouth?"

"Yes."

"Then ask for it."

"Death, I need your mouth. I need your lips. Please." Before she finished speaking he took one of her nipples into his mouth, sucking on the hard bud. She tasted fucking perfect. With his other hand, he gripped the flesh of her ass still covered in the jeans. When he first saw those jeans he'd thought they were hot with the way they molded to every curve of her body. Now, he hated the offending fabric. He wanted her naked, exposed, and ready for his cock.

Patience.

He was going to have to get used to that word. There was no chance of him forgetting himself. This was a side to Brianna he hadn't anticipated seeing so early. What had he done to draw her out? He wanted to know for future as he liked seeing her cheeks flushed with arousal. The needy look in her eyes would stay with him for a long time.

Moving to her other nipple, he sucked the hard bud into his mouth, groaning at the taste of her skin.

"Please, Death. I need you."

Licking between her breasts he circled each bud in turn. "I've got you, baby."

She cupped his face, pulling him away. Before he could protest her lips were on his and he was discovering a side to Brianna that he was loving.

Brianna's tongue plunged inside his mouth, and he met her tongue with his. Seconds later she pulled back, panting.

"Take your pants off," she said.

"I thought we weren't rushing?"

"I changed my mind." She tugged him to his feet.

Death chuckled going to the buckle of his belt.

Her gaze followed his movements. He loved having her eyes on his body. The arousal in her eyes was strong. Death wanted her to always look at him like that.

A knock at the door interrupted their moment.

"Dinner is going to be served soon," Pussy said, calling through the door.

"Fuck off," Death said, growling the word out to him.

Brianna glanced behind her looking as if the door was going to open at any minute. When he saw the handle being tried, Death lost it. Charging past her, he opened the door wide enough so Pussy only got to see him.

"Get the fuck out of my room," he said.

"Are you doing the hanky-panky with the lovely redhead?" Pussy asked.

Glaring at him, Death was close to killing the bastard. "If you still want to father children with your woman, get the fuck away now."

"What? I was only being kind to you. God, anyone would think I'm trying to irritate you. I was being nice. Brianna, tell him I was only being nice," Pussy said.

"Oh God," Brianna said.

"Fuck off." Death slammed the door closed, promising all kinds of hell when he got his hands on Pussy. His cock came before killing Pussy. Spinning around after locking the door he found Brianna sitting on the bed, laughing.

"Is he always like this?"

"Pussy's an asshole of the highest order. Bastard pisses me off."

At least she was laughing at Pussy's antics and not pissed by what he was doing. Standing in front of her with his belt open, Death stopped her from laughing.

"What do you want me to do now?" he asked.

****

When Pussy first started knocking on the door, she didn't know what to do. She was a little pissed off as he'd invaded the excitement of being with Death. Now, she stared up at Death, her man, and wondered what she should do.

Reaching out, she let her own desires take over rather than her fears. She didn't want to be controlled by fears. Death was the first man she'd ever wanted to be with. If she let her past fears control her, she wouldn't be able to move on to have a future.

She pulled the zipper down then dragged the jeans down with her.

His pants went down, and she was surprised to see he wasn't even wearing any underwear. The hard length of his cock sprang free, facing her. The tip of his cock was leaking pre-cum. The tiny droplet glistened in the light in the bedroom. She licked her lips, curious to know what his flavor would be. She wanted him, badly. In fact, she'd never wanted a man like she did Death.

Wrapping her fingers around his length, she gripped him tightly.

"Fuck, that feels good." He kept his hands at his side as she worked the length of his cock.

The more she worked the length the more pre-cum leaked out of the tip. With every jewel oozing out, she wanted to lick him, to taste him. In her mind she remembered the look on his face as the club whore gave him undeniable pleasure. She didn't want him to think of getting a blow job or anything else without thinking about her first.

"What are you thinking?" he asked. Glancing up the length of his body, she gave no answer. She didn't wear any bra or top, only wearing a pair of jeans. The entire experience was erotic, and she wanted it to last as long as possible. "The look in your eye, I want to keep it there. You look like you want to devour me."

"I don't want any other woman to think they can touch you. You're mine. You don't belong to anyone else."

She didn't have a clue where this sudden possessive instinct came from, but she wasn't going to share him with any other club women.

He was going to be all hers.

"Don't you worry, baby. I'm not the sharing kind of man. Some of the other brothers liked to do it once, but not me. I'm happy with one woman."

Brianna saw the truth in his eyes. Squeezing his shaft, she lowered her lips to the head and sucked on the tip. The salty taste of him hit her tongue, making her moan. He tasted so damn good. Exploring the tip, she swallowed all the pre-cum that exploded in her mouth.

"That's it, Brianna. Moan for me."

His hands were clenched by his sides. She knew all about the struggle of what to do, and so she took his hands, placing them in her hair.

"Touch me," she said, releasing his cock. She needed his hands on her as much as anything else. The desire he'd built inside her was not going to go away. Her nipples had always been sensitive to the touch. With him this close to her, it was only increasing.

Death sank his fingers into her hair, tightening in the strands.

"Your mouth is so damn good." He let out a little growl, pumping his hips into her mouth.

She opened her mouth a little wider to take more of him inside. The pleasure increased inside her.

"I want to lick your pussy, Brianna. Will you let

me?"

Pulling away from his cock, she stared up into his eyes.

"I'll make it feel so good. You're not going to know what hit you."

Could she do it? She'd be completely exposed to him.

The other night you were completely exposed to him and he made it so good.

She nodded her head, knowing she'd give him anything and all he needed to do was ask.

"Get on the bed."

"I still want to give you pleasure."

"I want those fantastic lips wrapped around my dick, baby. It's not going to change what I want."

Brianna lay on the bed where he asked her to. Her head ended up on the pillows while the rest of her was open for him. Death tugged his shirt off, removing his jeans completely and kicking off his boots. She watched him as he removed her boots then her jeans. She was naked apart from a small patch of material covering her pussy.

"This looks so fucking sexy. I'm going to remove it with my teeth."

She giggled, thinking how silly he was. There was no way he'd ever be able to remove the material with his teeth. The very idea was ludicrous.

"Never underestimate me, Brianna," he said. "I can prove you wrong more than once."

Raising a brow, she didn't say anything. There really was no need to offer him up a challenge he'd never be able to complete.

"Don't believe me?" he asked.

Shaking her head, she rested her hands beside her head. "Prove it."

What had happened to her? There was a time when she'd be completely terrified of the challenge he offered.

The other women. You can't let him go with other women.

She didn't want to lose her place by his side. It was selfish and stupid, but it was something she was going to have to live with. When it came to Death, she was utterly jealous of someone else getting his attention.

His fingers skimmed up the outside of her thigh, working up to get to her pussy. He didn't touch her panties with his fingers. Death withdrew his touch from her, moving to lie flush on the bed.

"I want to touch you as well," she said, meaning every word she spoke.

"You will get a chance, baby. For now, I'm going to prove to you that I can take these panties off you without any help from my hands."

He gripped the tops of her thighs and opened her legs wide. She moaned at his touch, watching his gaze wander down her body to rest directly over her pussy. "You don't see what I do, baby. I see how beautiful these red curls look, wet and slick from your cream."

"How can you see them? I'm wearing panties."

"I see them."

She giggled, loving the way he was making her feel.

"Okay, I'll believe you." She didn't, not one bit.

His lips went to the inside of her left thigh, making her freeze up. In the next second she felt his tongue on her thigh going up to her pussy. He was sticking to his own rules as his hands glided up her body to cup her breasts. Death pinched her nipples as his tongue teased the lace of her panties.

Brianna gasped as his tongue slid underneath the

material, gathering the fabric up in his teeth. She bit her lip trying to contain her groans of pleasure at his touch.

He moved the fabric out of the way and tugged. The flimsy fabric snapped away from her body. She looked down to see the material in his mouth like that of a dog with a bone.

"I told you," he said, taking the material out of his mouth. He threw the offending item away, smiling at her. "Now, I can really see your pussy."

"You couldn't before?"

"No, but I sure could fucking imagine it. I can tell you, baby, the sight in front of me is nothing like I imagined. It's so much fucking better." He opened the lips of her sex, spreading her wide.

Brianna cried out as his tongue flicked over her clit, driving her crazy with need. He moved down, plundering her cunt, fucking her as if his fingers were a cock. She gripped the blanket beneath her for something to hold on to. Nothing felt steady to her anymore. There was no control in her actions. This was what it meant to belong to Death, to be controlled by the pleasure of his mouth.

"Let me hear you scream for me," he said.

She gave over to the pleasure he was creating, letting him hear everything he was doing.

You should be licking him now.

"I want to taste you." It was hard for her to talk to him as he was creating the most amazing pleasure with her body.

He glanced up at her. "Are you sure?"

The blonde giving him a blow job entered her mind. "Yes, I'm totally sure."

Death changed positions so that she was facing his cock. The tip was still leaking pre-cum, and she missed the taste of him in her mouth.

"I'm going to lick you, and even when you come the first time I'm not going to stop."

She doubted he'd give her multiple orgasms. There was no doubt he'd at least give her one, but multiple, not a chance. She didn't believe he was capable of such a feat.

Brianna didn't say anything to contradict what he said. If he believed he could give her multiple orgasms, who was she to contradict him?

She gripped his length once again, pulling up to take him inside her mouth.

"Fuck." The curse exploded out in the air, echoing off the walls, thrilling her with its ferocity.

Circling the head, she sucked him into her mouth, loving the taste of him on her tongue. She'd never get bored of this. His tongue attacked her clit, causing her stomach to clench at the orgasm drawing closer. Her stomach grew tighter as he circled her clit. The tightening ball of need exploded inside her, making her desperate for him. Two fingers fucked inside her, tipping her over the edge into bliss.

Brianna sucked more of his dick into her mouth, moaning as he hit the back of her throat. It didn't stop there as she took more of him, swallowing him down. Her orgasm drew her to the edge, wanting to take Death along with her.

"I'm not going to last," he said.

She didn't care. Death pushed her into a second orgasm as she claimed her first from him, swallowing down his load. Brianna listened as he grunted out his pleasure. She was more than pleased with her victory.

He pulled out of her mouth, turning around to collapse beside her.

"Fuck me, baby. I'll never look at another woman's lips again."

Smiling, she snuggled up to him. She was more than happy for him to stick with her.

Chapter Nine

One week later and the snowstorm that had been threatened for the course of December had finally hit. It was five days until the big day, and Death was fucking excited. He'd not been this excited since he was a little boy. The clubhouse looked like a bunch of cartoon characters had been at it. Usually it would have bothered him to have the clubhouse looking like a fun house. This year, after Gonzalez, Ashley, and all the shit that had come to them, Death found it refreshing to be inside. The kids were lapping it up, but now, they were only taking necessary trips out to the town. It was far too dangerous to be risking your life for a quick trip. There was a large list stuck to the refrigerator for them to add to. No one was leaving until the last of the items were finished. He didn't mind. It was fun being around the clubhouse with Brianna. The men, including Dick, had all backed off. None of them were trying to take her away from him, which he was more than happy about.

He'd fight every single one of his brothers, even Devil, if one denied her in his life. Devil had the right to stop one of the women becoming an old lady. He had almost done it to Sasha. If it wasn't for Pussy then Death doubted if Devil would have allowed it.

There was no tension in the air, and it made for an enjoyable living. While the mornings were brilliant, his nights were fucking amazing. Brianna didn't like the thought of another woman giving him what she couldn't. He hadn't been lying to her as he didn't mind waiting for what he wanted. They'd not fucked, but they'd done a lot of touching, exploring, and bringing each other to orgasm. Over the last week he'd gotten her used to being naked around him. She'd finally slept naked against him the night before last. He wouldn't let her wear any clothes in bed anymore. This morning he'd woken up to find her curled up around him. His dick protested at the close contact, being so close to her and not being able to touch.

This morning when she'd woken up to see the state that she'd put him in, Brianna had brought him off with her hand, watching his white cum spill onto his stomach. He'd been totally surprised as she rested his spent cock on his stomach. She'd whispered good morning to him, leaving the bed and him in shock.

Not to be outdone, Death had gone searching for her in the shower. He didn't let her leave until he'd brought her to two orgasms, one with his fingers, the other with his mouth.

Feeling accomplished, he'd left the room, giving her space to get ready to come down.

Sipping at his coffee, Death now waited for her to come inside. She didn't make an appearance straight away. Snake entered first looking damn happy about himself.

"Date night?" Death asked.

"Yep. I get to prove to the little snippy nurse that I'm not a complete scumbag." Snake cricked his neck, letting out a sigh. "It's a beautiful day to fuck someone new."

"You *are* a scumbag," Mia said, entering the kitchen. "Everyone knows you're a scumbag. This nurse will as well."

"How do you know about my nurse?"

"Judi told me. She tells me everything."

Shaking his head, Death burst out laughing at Snake's curse.

"Devil, old ladies have turned this place into a fucking spa where they can talk about girly shit. It's time we took this place back." Snake glared at all the women.

Death perked up as he saw his own woman entering the room. Her cheeks went a wonderful shade of red when she caught sight of him. Smirking, he raised his cup in greeting.

"What about you, red? Do you think I'm a scumbag?"

"I don't know you."

Snake was silent for several minutes without speaking. "You're red, red."

Brianna's gaze found his.

"Leave her alone, Snake. She's mine."

"I don't want her, even though she's sexy as hell in those jeans. I'd fuck her, though, if you're not going to."

Brianna went even redder, but Death wasn't amused by his comments about his woman. "I suggest you shut the fuck up if you want to be capable of going on a date and doing anything about it." He got up from his position from the table, ready to commit murder if he had to.

"Back off, Death. I'm not going to touch your woman," Snake said.

"Where are you going for the big date?" Mia asked.

"I don't know. I'll think of something."

"It's snowing. There's nothing more romantic than snow," Mia said, sighing. "I love the snow."

"I know you do," Curse said, entering the room, "which is why we're going to have some fun later. I've got plans." He moved toward Mia, kissing her hard before grabbing a coffee.

Death had missed this, the hustle and bustle of the club that surrounded him.

"I love you," Mia said, speaking the words aloud.

Death looked toward Brianna, wondering what

she thought about listening to Mia's confession of love.

Do you want love?

I don't do love.

Now I do love.

Shit, what the fuck is going on?

Brianna moved past him, brushing up against him as she went. He watched her grabbing the coffee pot and a mug. Death didn't look away from her ass as she leaned over to get the sugar. His cock hardened further at the sight of her.

Their nights were never enough. He always wanted more with her, but he wouldn't take it too far until she was ready for more. Returning his gaze to Snake, he saw the other man looked deeply troubled.

"You're not going to get into her pants if you're a pussy about it," Mia said.

"I'm not trying to get into her pussy." Snake looked at all of them. "Fuck you all. You're all doing it on purpose."

Everyone burst out laughing at Snake's expression.

"No, all joking aside, you've got to find something to do for your date. You can't expect her to make her own fun," Mia said.

Snake stormed out of the room.

"Poor guy. He really doesn't have the first clue what's coming to him, does he?" Mia asked. "What's this nurse like?"

"She's hot, sassy, and everything Snake needs to keep him grounded," Judi said, entering with Ripper. The other woman looked a little green around the gills.

"Are you okay?" Death asked, concerned for the other woman.

"I'm fine, just feeling tired. I can't wait for her to be born." She rubbed her stomach, smiling.

"Her?" Brianna asked.

"We didn't ask to learn the sex, but Judi seems to think we're having a girl." Ripper rubbed Judi's shoulders, lovingly.

"She'll be here before you know it," Lexie said, rubbing her own stomach. "Believe me, I've had two already."

Judi chuckled. "Just because you've had two doesn't mean you're any better at it."

"I don't know. I know more than most women," Lexie said, laughing.

Death had had enough. Taking hold of Brianna's hands, he led the way out of the room getting them some privacy.

"What are you doing?" she asked.

"They'll start talking about pregnancy, vomit, shit, girly things, I can't take it." He found a room without anyone in it. It just happened to be the cinema room. This was where members could come and watch television, without any of the other mundane crap. Since Brianna had been in residence the place had shone brighter than ever before. "Also, I just wanted to get you alone." He tugged her down onto his lap as he took the first seat he came to.

"Why?"

"The club can get a little full on. It only makes sense for me to get you alone while I can." He rubbed his nose along her cheek going to her neck. His possessive instinct had taken over when it came to Brianna.

"I missed you," she said, turning her face toward him.

Brianna kissed him first, plunging her tongue into his mouth. He moaned, sinking his fingers into her red hair, holding her in place.

"I love your lips on me," he said, groaning.

"Me, too." She cupped his face, deepening their kiss. Death's cock was rock hard, and it got even harder as she reached down between them to touch him. His shaft hardened even more in her hand.

"You had me in your hands this morning, and it still wasn't enough."

"It's never enough," she said, gasping as he sucked at the pulse beside her neck.

"All you've got to do is say the words." He wouldn't push. This was entirely on her.

"I want you, Death. I want to fuck you. I want to have it all with you."

He froze at her words as they were unexpected. "Do you want to wait?"

"No, I want you now. Please, Death, take me back to our room and fuck me," she said.

There was no need to tell him twice. Picking her up in his arms, he carried her out of the room up the stairs. They passed Pussy, Sasha, and her dog on the way.

"What's going on?" Pussy asked.

"Nothing." Death didn't stop not even when Sasha asked what was going on. His main mission was to get to his room and naked.

"You don't have to rush," Brianna said, giggling.

It had become a long standing joke between the two of them about rushing. Neither of them wanted to rush, and yet both of them when they got started, craved each other. Death had never felt like this for another woman, and he was starting to fear the reason why. When it came to Brianna he'd started to fall for her and not just for the sex. He loved her company and missed her constantly when they were no longer together. His nights and mornings were the best part of his life. Being around her thrilled him. He didn't need anything else other than her smile.

You're turning into a pussy like the others.

Slamming the door closed behind him, he lowered her to her feet, giving her one last chance to push him away.

You're in love with her.

Before he did, he claimed one last kiss.

****

Brianna had wanted to take their passion to the next level yet held herself back from taking that other step. When his lips claimed hers, all doubt vanished from her mind. She wanted him more than anything. This was what she'd been needing for a long time since she first met him.

She'd seen the club whores trying to get his attention. Death didn't pay them any mind. Now he cupped her face, sliding his tongue over her lips, and she opened up to allow him inside.

"Choose, Brianna." He whispered the words against her lips.

"I've already made a decision. I want you, Death. I'm not going to back down." She stepped away from him, missing his touch the moment she did. Grabbing the bottom of her shirt, she tugged it over her head, watching as Death did the same. His ink stood out once again across his chest and down his abs. He made her mouth water. All she wanted to do was lick him, taste him, and remember him for herself.

"That look I'm going to keep on your face," he said.

"What look?"

He reached out, sinking his fingers into her hair. She loved it when he did that, gripping her hair tightly. Death controlled her movements, and she gave him the control. This wasn't being taken from her. He asked her permission every step of the way without even asking the words. Even as he held her, she knew if she stepped back and shook her head, he'd release her instantly. That alone kept her grounded.

She was safe with him. This time she didn't want to take a step back. Looking into his eyes, she tugged on the buckle of his jeans. She'd sucked him off a couple of times, loving the taste of him as he exploded in her mouth.

"You're so beautiful, Brianna."

"You're only saying that because I'm about to get your cock out."

He slammed his lips down on hers cutting off any more dirty talk. Death nibbled on her lips. Not once did he stop her as she pushed his pants down far enough to grip the length of his cock.

Death hissed. "Be careful, baby. I'm desperate to be inside your tight little pussy."

Squeezing the root of his cock, she moved up to run her thumb over the slit. His pre-cum coated her thumb, and she brought it to her lips, sucking it off.

"I don't know how you can ever doubt who I belong to. None of the club whores have anything on you." He whispered the words against her temple. Death took her hand, pressing it against his chest. "You're in here."

She didn't say anything, only looked at him. What was she to say? Brianna settled on what they were doing now. She didn't want to assume anything from his actions.

"Fuck me, Death."

He turned her around, pressing her down to the bed like he had the other day. She loved it when he took control, not giving her a chance to argue with him. There was nothing more erotic to her than Death showing how much he desired her. His touch, the way he talked, all of it reminded her that she was in the present, with him, and nothing could hurt her. The bad memories of the past were few and far between with him in her life. Whenever she thought about anything bad, she focused her thoughts on Death, and all of her fears disappeared.

"I'm going to fuck you so damn good you're not going to remember anyone else."

With his arms wrapped around her, she didn't need to remember anyone else. There was only one person for her, and that was Death.

She unbuttoned her jeans, working them down her hips as Death took over pulling them all the way down her body. Her panties followed until she lay before him on the bed naked.

"I don't want to wear a condom."

"Okay."

"Are you on any birth control?"

"No."

"We'll deal with it when it happens."

There was no fear inside her at his words, only acceptance. She was more than happy to deal with whatever problems they had together.

You're falling in love with him.

No, she didn't think she was falling in love with him—she knew she was in love with him. Death had sneaked past all of her cold defenses, and now there was nothing left but to accept what had happened.

"What?" he asked.

"Nothing. It's all fine." She wasn't about to tell him her revelation. All of it would come out in the open with time.

She licked her lips as he stood up, removing his jeans completely. His cock was long, thick, and leaking pre-cum out of the tip. She'd never known a man to have so much pre-cum, and even when she swallowed his release, there was copious amounts of the stuff.

He crawled onto the bed, opening her thighs as he went. "First, I'm going to lick this beautiful pussy before I stick my cock inside you."

Brianna cried out as his tongue flicked her clit. He teased her with the wickedness of his tongue. She gripped the blanket beneath trying to hold onto something, hoping her sanity could take the pleasure.

Death moved down to plunge his tongue within her cunt, fucking her repeatedly. She knew it wouldn't feel anything like the thick length of his cock.

"Going to get you nice and wet for me."

She was dripping wet. Brianna felt how slick she was as her cream slid down to coat her anus. Crying out, she stared up at the ceiling in the hope of finding some strength to hold off her orgasm.

"Don't fight me, baby. You're only going to torture yourself. I can go all day and night." He flicked her clit repeatedly until she had no fight left within her.

Screaming, she felt the flow of her release overtake her. There was nothing else she could do. Her stomach tightened as the pleasure increased. He sucked her clit into his mouth hard, drawing the last of the pleasure out of her.

Death moved up her body, smiling down at her. "I could eat your pussy all day long."

"I'll remember that," she said.

He smiled. The wickedness had things once again tightening inside her. "Tell me if you want me to stop."

She didn't want him to stop. Gazing down the length of their bodies, she watched the tip of his cock tease her entrance. Brianna gasped as the wide length of his head spread her open wide. When the tip was inside her, he returned his hand to hers. He gripped both of her hands, pressing them up beside her head, holding her in place.

Staring into his eyes, she felt the rock hard length of him as he thrust in deep. Screaming out, she closed her eyes only to have him order her not to.

"Keep those eyes on me," he said. "I'm the one fucking you, Brianna. No one else, only me."

Opening her eyes she stared back at him.

"That's it, I'm the one inside you. I'm the one fucking you."

She winced as he fucked the last few inches inside her. He was rock hard and very deep, hitting her cervix.

"Sh, it's okay. You've got all of me." The tenderness in his voice brought tears to her eyes. "I've got you. Who's inside you?"

"Death, you're inside me." She didn't need these reassurances, yet she was touched by them.

He tightened his hold on her hands, holding her down. When he was ready, he pulled up and slowly began to thrust in and out of her. It started out very slow where she felt every little inch of him within her, spreading her open.

"Please, Death, fuck me." She began to beg him, needing him to fuck his way inside her. The ache building inside her was painful, and she needed the relief he could provide.

"Are you ready for me?"

"Yes."

Death released her hands gripping one of her hips as the other held up the rest of his body.

He fucked her hard and furiously, filling her pussy to the hilt until there was nothing left for him to fuck her with. She thrust up to meet him, loving the build of pleasure from his hands.

"You're so fucking tight, baby. I love fucking your pussy. I don't want to be anywhere else but inside you, fucking you." He leaned down to claim her lips. Brianna opened up to him. There was no way she was fighting this burning need inside her. "I can feel you tightening, getting ready to come. I want to feel you explode around my cock, squeezing me."

She couldn't look away from him as he spoke. What he was saying hypnotized her with his words.

"So fucking tight and hot. I could be inside you all the fucking time." He growled the words against her neck making her shiver.

"Yes, Death, please."

"Touch your clit. Let me feel you come."

Reaching down between their bodies, she began to touch her clit, stroking the nub. The sensation was strange with the hard length of him fucking her hard as she played with herself. He pounded inside, and she kept touching her clit. With each thrust inside her he bumped her hand against her pussy, making contact each time. She loved the way he touched her, drawing her closer and closer to orgasm.

"Fuck, baby, I can't last."

Before he finished, he thrust her into an earth shattering climax, her second of the night.

"Fuck, yeah. I can feel your tight pussy clenching me like a fist." He slammed harder inside her, going as deep as he could get. She'd never felt anything so totally amazing in her life.

He thrust one final time, and she felt him jerk inside her, exploding within her core. His cum pulsed deep inside her, claiming her, owning her. Brianna knew she wasn't ever going to be the same again.

****

That night Snake stood outside of the diner

waiting for Jessica to come to him. She wouldn't let him meet her at home and arranged to meet here. He was smoking while watching the people coming and going. It was fucking freezing, and he stood in his leather jacket waiting for her to arrive.

His cell phone went off, and he placed his smoke between his lips, searching his pockets. "What?" he asked without looking at the caller.

"How's your date going?" Judi asked.

"You're phoning up to check up on me?" He turned to look up and down the street. There was still no sign of Jessica. No woman had ever stood him up before, and he refused to believe she would today.

"I wanted to see how the date is going."

"She hasn't arrived." He hated admitting that little truth to her. What pissed him off the most was the fact he was still standing out, waiting.

"She hasn't? That's a first for you, right?"

"Yes." He admitted the truth between gritted teeth.

Judi laughed, and he was sure he heard Mia, Lexie, and Sasha in the background.

"You're all fucking priceless," he said, growling out the words.

Get a fucking move on. Stop waiting around for the bitch.

Throwing his cigarette to the ground, he stumped it out, and stormed off. He'd find the first available woman and lose all of his frustrations all at once.

"The Snake is no longer deadly. No one wants you to inject venom into their vajayjay," Judi said, laughing.

Closing the phone, he pocketed the device even though all he wanted to actually do was throw the blasted thing away. He was pissed off, cold, horny, and downright disappointed, which scared him more. Snake didn't look forward to other women's company, yet he wanted Jessica's company.

"Snake?"

He turned to see Jessica walking down the street. She only wore a light jacket, and even from the low light cast down from the lamps, he saw she wore her scrubs.

"If you were going to stand me up you shouldn't have fucking agreed." He didn't move an inch from where he stood.

Jessica stopped in front of him, panting. In the cold he saw her cheeks were flushed.

"I didn't have your number, and when I tried to ask Lydia for it, she refused." Jessica stopped, holding a hand out for him to stop. "I need to catch my breath." She stood, bent forward, then stood tall again. "Fuck me, I've not run that fast since I was in high school well over ten years ago."

"How old are you?" he asked, amused by her.

"Twenty-eight." She blew some of her raven hair that had fallen over her face. "I can't let any patients know how unfit I am. It would be so hard telling them to get fit when I can't even run." She held her sides, smiling at him. "Right, I couldn't get in touch with you. I don't know where you live. I'm sort of out of the loop on your biker gang. You're like some secret society that no one talks about."

"We're a club. Chaos Bleeds," he said.

"I heard. I just don't think it's important to remember."

"We're a pretty important club. Popular, too."

"Yeah, you're popular for screwing around on women. Fucking them, leaving them, it doesn't exactly get my juices flowing, if you know what I mean. Besides, I've got a hell of a lot more important crap to remember than your little gang." Both of her hands were on her hips.

"Why not? I can get those juices flowing exactly how you need." He decided not to be offended by her gang comment.

She shook her head. "You're completely insane. Anyway, I couldn't get in touch, and I wanted to apologize. I've been called into the hospital. They need extra hands tonight. The snow, the roads, it's causing a lot of accidents and a lot of falls. I've got to go."

"You agreed to a date." The thought of finding another woman didn't thrill him.

"I know I agreed, but there's nothing I can do. I can't stop accidents from happening. They need me, and I've got a duty to go."

"How long will you be?" Snake asked.

"I don't know. It could be half the night or longer."

"I'll wait for you."

"What?" she asked.

"I'll come and sit in the hospital, waiting. We made a deal. You either renege on our deal and all bets are off, or you allow me to wait and we have a date. I don't care what time it is. I've got nothing better to do."

Are you crazy? There are a lot of available women out there who want you.

"Sure, if you don't mind waiting. You didn't exactly strike me as the kind of man to wait around. I'm not a sure thing. I won't be having sex with you."

"I'm not going to be having sex with you either." *Even though I really want to.* He didn't add the last part. When it came to Jessica, baby steps needed to be taken.

"Okay, erm, sure, follow me."

"I got my bike."

"I know. I parked beside you." He followed her

around to the parking lot, expecting to see some pussy car that didn't do over the speed limit, which he recalled seeing her in before. Snake paused as he saw another top of the range bike, resting beside his own. This bike was black with pink stripes along the sides.

"Where's your car?"

"I didn't say I drove here. I said I was parked beside you." She stepped beside her machine.

"You like bikes?"

"I've got a license to ride a bike, so I guess I like bikes. Who knew?" She smiled at him. "Follow me to the hospital."

He climbed on his bike, admiring her body as she straddled her machine. She looked fucking sexy. He wanted to fuck her, and Snake decided to make that his mission.

Chapter Ten

Death left the room long enough to grab some food. He found Dick sitting at the large table, eating ice cream. There were at least six different tubs in front of him.

"What are you doing?" Death asked.

"I figured women do this all the time. I thought I'd give it a try and see if it works." Dick scooped a large piece and ate it.

"You didn't have a thing for Brianna."

"You're right. I didn't. I just wanted to fuck her and piss you off. I've got to get my kicks somewhere."

Death stayed still, clenching his hand rather than giving in to the desire to hurt the bastard in front of him. All Dick was trying to do was start a fight, and he refused to bite. He wouldn't give the other man the sick sense of pleasure he'd get from riling him.

"What? You're not going to beat the shit out of me?"

"You're not worth it."

"So I'm not worth it now even though if Brianna came to me, I'd still fuck her?" Dick licked some ice cream off his spoon, grinning wickedly at Death.

"You know what? Fuck you, Dick. I've done absolutely nothing to you, and yet you're being a dick. Fuck you, and fuck your attitude."

Death turned his back on the other man, grabbing some food from the fridge. He picked anything that they could eat with their fingers, which included a lot of cold meats that had been cooked. Everything in the fridge was made by at least one of the women. There was even a heavenly chocolate fudge cake in the back with instructions to leave alone. He pulled it out, taking two large slices.

"You're right. I didn't want her, but I didn't want to make anything easy," Dick said.

Death turned to look at Dick, who was still eating ice cream. "Why?"

"I've lost anything of any value to me. I'm sick and tired of living without any of the excitement anymore."

"You were a drug addict and drank too fucking much. What the hell was there to love? What the fuck are you missing?"

"The high. I miss the high that I got. This life, it's not fucking fun. The sweet-butts are nothing but whores. I'm sick and tired of the same old shit. I hate Christmas, the women, all of it. I've got to get my high some way. You're not giving it to me."

Death shook his head. "You know they send people like you to asylums away from living life."

"I'm not crazy."

"No, you just need your fix. What's stopping you? You hate the club, you hate living here, life is shit, what's the fucking problem?" Death asked, so over this shit.

"This club is the only thing I've got left."

"Then I suggest you start acting like it," Devil said, walking into the room. He was carrying Elizabeth on his hip. Their president wore a pair of sweat pants and nothing else. "I'm sick of dealing with your shit. You can act like a dick in your own time, not in mine. I'm not interested in whatever's going on in your life. No drugs, and no more destructive behavior. We've got kids to think about."

Devil went to the fridge grabbing the medicine from the drawer.

Death decided to leave Devil to handle Dick's shit. He wasn't interested in anything that had to be said.

Taking his plate full of bounty back up to his room, Death entered to find Brianna flicking through the channels. She wore the shirt he'd been wearing earlier and looked totally hot in his clothes. Kicking his door shut, locking it, he handed her the large plate. "I took whatever I could find."

"I'm starving."

They'd spent the entire day in his bedroom, neither of them venturing out even as Pussy knocked on the door to inform them dinner was ready. There was nothing sane about that bastard. He got more fun from invading other people's space.

"I saw Dick in the kitchen."

"What about him?" she asked, taking a chunk of meat. He loved her appetite. It reminded him of his own. Death was hungry after spending all day fucking her.

"He's feeling sorry for himself, missing all of his highs from addiction. Devil won't allow it anymore. The club needs to stay clean. We can all drink but nothing else."

"Did you ever do drugs?"

"I did drugs, but I never took to them. I hated the lack of control. There was nothing fun or exciting about it. I didn't get anything from it other than problems. I wasn't going to change for them. Dick, he took them quickly, like Butler. They were both hard partiers. For a long time they were useless to the club."

"I can't imagine them being part of the club if they didn't have any uses at all."

"They had their uses when needed. Over time, they'd just become a problem. Shit happened, we needed to change, and we did." Death shrugged, taking a piece of cheese for himself. He'd never thought he could get used to this. They were becoming familiar with each other.

Death knew the truth. He was in love with her, and this was how he got close to her all the time. Being inside her just cemented his feelings. He wanted her swollen and pregnant with his kid. There was nothing else that would give him greater pleasure than to have her in his life, pregnant with his kid.

"I was thinking after Christmas we could get out own place," he said.

Brianna looked at him. "Are you sure?"

"Yeah. I know how I feel about you. I'm not going to change who I am."

"I don't want you to change."

"The only question remains, do you want to spend the rest of your life with me?"

"Yes, I do." There was no hesitation in her voice.

"Then we'll start looking."

Brianna took the plate from his hands, placing it on the drawer cabinet beside his bed. She straddled his lap, pulling the shirt from her body, exposing her tits to his gaze. Not one word was spoken as she cupped his cheek, drawing his lips to hers as she deepened the kiss. Her tongue glided over his lips, going inside. Death sank his fingers into the length of her hair, groaning as she ground her naked cunt over his covered cock. He had kept the sweat pants on when he handed her the food. The television played to itself. His only focus was on the full, ripe woman in his arms.

"I want you, Death."

With her on his lap, he shuffled their positions to move his pants down his legs to the floor. "Then take what you want, baby. I'm more than happy to comply."

She gripped his cock in her fist, smoothing over the tip. Brianna didn't keep him waiting long as she lifted up, aligned the tip to her entrance, and slid down.

He groaned at the exquisite pleasure of her tight

heat surrounding him. "I can't get over how tight you are," he said.

"Do you always talk dirty?"

"You think that's dirty? You've seen nothing yet." He released her hair to grip the curve of her ass. Death pulled her down to take more of his cock. "I can show you exactly what dirty means."

She leaned forward, sucking on his neck. "Then show me dirty."

Using the grip he had on her hips, he lifted her up and slammed her back down, forcing her to take more of his cock. She cried out, whimpering as he repeated the action several times. Her tits bounced in front of his face.

"I can feel how tight you are from this angle. I'm going to fuck you so damn hard you're not going to know where I end and you begin."

She gripped his shoulders, sinking her nails into his flesh.

"I'm going to have you begging me to let you come."

Her green eyes were filled with desperation. When he'd had enough of taking her hot pussy with her astride him, he tugged her off.

"Remember, whenever you want me to stop, tell me."

Death placed her on her knees before him, sliding back inside her. "How about this?" This angle made him deeper, stroking over her g-spot. He stared at her puckered anus. He caressed her clit, using her lube to wet his fingers. Death brought his fingers back to her forbidden channel and pressed.

She tensed up around him.

"Do you want me to stop?" he asked.

"No. I want you to continue. I don't want you to stop." She sounded breathless. He loved the sounds coming from her throat. For the rest of the night he was going to be driving her wild with his touch.

****

Brianna groaned as he continued to stroke her ass. She'd never really liked her ass being played with. Death's touch only turned her on even more.

"Relax for me," he said.

The size of his cock stretched her, filling her to the brink on the verge of pain. His fingers playing with her anus didn't help. She wanted to push back against him to take more of his fingers inside her ass.

He pressed one finger harder against her ass, pushing past the tight ring of muscle. The moment he got past she breathed a sigh of relief. "I'm going to fuck your ass very soon, Brianna. You're going to be begging for it."

She was already begging for it. Brianna didn't know what she wanted more, his cock in her pussy or in her ass.

"That's what you want, isn't it, baby?"

"Yes." She wasn't going to lie to him or argue. When it came to Death, she wanted to give it all to him.

She'd already figured when she was going to tell him how she felt. There was a reason Christmas was a time for giving. She was going to give Death what she'd never given any other man before in her life, her heart. When it came to Death, she truly wanted to be everything he was hunting for.

He slowed his thrusts and stroked at her anus, pressing a second finger inside her. Death began to press inside her, going in deep as he worked up a pattern with his fingers. "Yeah, I'm going to fuck this little ass and make it mine. I'm going to love every part of you, Brianna."

"Yes. I want you so much, Death." No one else

could ever give her the kind of pleasure Death did. There was something powerful between them that went a hell of a lot stronger than mere attraction. She wanted this to last, to draw him even closer to her. If she was pregnant, she wouldn't be scared but happy by the sudden turn of events. The thought of having his child filled her with joy.

"That's right, I do." He began to increase his thrusts going deeper than ever before. "Take all of me, Brianna. Take my cock and my fingers."

She whimpered as he took her hard and with force. There was no waiting around as Death claimed her completely.

"I'm going to fill your pussy up with my cum, and then I'm going to take this ass."

There was no holding back as he pounded inside her. She was so close to another orgasm as he began to saw his fingers in her ass.

"I can feel your cunt getting ready to explode. You want me to let you come, Brianna?" he asked.

"Yes." She bit her lip trying to contain her squeals of excitement.

"You're so fucking wet. I can see you dripping around my cock. I'm covered in your cum, baby."

She groaned at his dirty talk.

The hand that had been resting on her hip, slid between her thighs to touch her clit.

"Fuck yourself back against me. Take my cock while I bring you off."

Brianna did as he asked, pushing herself back against him.

"You've got such a tight cunt. My tight cunt."

He stroked her clit, and it only took a couple of strokes for her to reach orgasm. Within seconds he gripped her hip with one hand, slamming inside her. He was relentless in his pursuit, and she loved every second of it.

"Fuck, baby. Take it all." Death plunged inside her one final time. His cock jerked inside her, exploding his cum deep into her womb.

Will this produce a baby?

She didn't know what it would produce, only that she wasn't scared at the prospect of becoming a mother.

Collapsing to the bed, she let out a sigh. Death moved to her side, panting. "Fuck, baby, that was perfect." He reached over, kissing her cheek. "Stay here. I'll go and get cleaned up."

Brianna didn't move. She stayed still with her ass in the air, no longer caring about her exposed self.

He returned seconds later holding a cloth. "I think it's time to clean you up." Death placed the cloth against her ass, wiping.

"What about your cum?" she asked, confused as to why he'd start with her ass first.

"I'm not wiping myself away. I love seeing my seed spill from the lips of your pussy. It's so fucking sexy to watch. I wish you could see how fucking amazing you look filled with my cum."

He slapped her ass making her yelp. Rolling over, she sat up, glaring at him. He was laughing. "I thought that would get your attention."

"That hurt."

"No, it didn't." He cupped her face, and she pulled away wrinkling her nose.

"You better have cleaned your fingers."

"Of course I did." He cupped her face once again, drawing her closer to him. Death took possession of her lips, licking along her bottom lip. "Perfect."

She watched him throw the towel into the corner near their clothes. He settled down on the bed, pulling her into his arms.

Brianna closed her eyes, basking in the feel of him surrounding her.

"When we get our own place will you still want to come to the club?" he asked.

"Our place?"

"Yeah, I'm not going to force you or any children we have to remain here."

"Do you think I'm going to stay here with you?" she asked, teasing.

"If you weren't, you wouldn't be here now. I know you want me, Brianna."

"Or your cock."

"Or my cock." He chuckled, dropping a kiss to her cheek. "In all seriousness, would you still want to come to the clubhouse?"

"This is your home, Death. Your family is here. You love it here, and if I'm being honest, I love it here. Well, I like cleaning your mess. I don't know why, but I've always loved cleaning. It helps to calm and soothe me."

"I noticed. I've also noticed you like to cook as well."

"I know my uncle caused you and the club a lot of pain—"

He cut her off before she said anything more.

"Gonzalez caused us a lot of pain. Ronald ruined part of your life. The pain is equal, baby. I promise you, I don't hold a grudge, and neither does the club. I've claimed you as my old lady, and it makes you mine. They respect it."

She breathed out a sigh, feeling the tears well up in her eyes. "You really mean that?" she asked.

"Of course I mean it. It's a damn promise."

"Then I'd love for us to get our own place, but

I'll still come here to clean. Without me this place would be a mess."

"Lexie, Mia, and Judi would be pissed if they heard you saying that."

"They're rarely at the clubhouse usually. I've heard them. They only come here for special occasions."

"That's true," he said.

"Also, June and the others, they're useless at cleaning. The only thing they know how to do is vacuum up cock." She glared recalling the blonde with her lips around Death.

Death, in response, burst out laughing. "You're completely insane, and I love it."

He didn't stop laughing.

Feeling silly, Brianna joined him, loving how easy it was and safe to be with him.

Tell him.

No, she wasn't going to tell him. She had decided when would be the best time to tell Death that she loved him. Now wasn't the time.

"I love hearing you laugh."

"It's fun to laugh again."

Death reached over her, grabbing the remote. "Let's see what's on the television."

"Okay."

She settled down with her head on his lap, watching as he picked something for them to both watch. This was what she'd been wanting for as long as she could remember. Love, sexual attraction, belonging, she wanted all of it, and she knew in her heart of hearts that she'd get it with this man.

****

Snake watched Jessica come and go. He didn't understand why he was still sitting in the emergency room waiting for her to finish.

Any bitch could take care of your needs.

The door kept opening as more people fucked over parts of their body because of the snow.

His cell phone went off, and he pulled it out, seeing it was the clubhouse.

"What?" he asked, annoyed that he was still sitting in the same place even though he could have any woman he wanted.

"Hey, baby. I'm missing you," June said.

Jessica chose that moment to come out. She spoke to the woman on the reception, and he watched her fringe puff out as she exhaled. The woman was tired, yet she took another file.

"Are you listening to me?" When he was faced with the raven haired beauty, June lost all of her appeal. The club whore wasn't what he wanted. No, he wanted the nurse who was making her way toward him.

"I've got to go." He hung up, knowing Jessica would be pissed to find him talking to another woman while waiting for her.

What does it matter? She's only a woman who's not related to the club.

"Hey," Jessica said. "Look, I understand if you want to leave. I'm more than happy for you to go if you want. This is taking longer than I expected."

"I don't mind waiting. I'm still here."

"Okay. So long as you don't mind."

"I don't mind."

The night wore on, and around two in the morning Snake fell asleep until someone shook him awake.

"What time is it?" he asked, stretching. He'd fallen asleep sat in the chair, and his back was killing him. He'd not been this uncomfortable since moving to Piston County.

"It's six in the morning," Jessica said. "I can go. We can have breakfast if you want."

He stood up, clearing the sleep from his eyes. "Sure."

"You're pretty persistent."

"You promised me a date. I'm not going anywhere until I get that date." He followed her outside to where their bikes were parked.

"Well, I'm surprised. I kept expecting to see you gone every time I came to the reception area. When I saw you sleeping, I figured I'd leave you."

"I've not slept like that in years. Oh well, there was nothing better to do." He'd enjoyed watching her appear and disappear taking new patients through.

"I'm really sorry."

"No, it's dangerous, and I understand."

"I never thought you would. I'm off now though. We'll have breakfast, and then I'm going to sleep for the day."

She put the helmet on.

"I'll meet you at the diner," he said.

Snake waited for her to leave first before climbing on his bike.

He didn't think about the reason he kept following her or why he stayed at the hospital.

You want her pussy.

No, it was more than that. So many women had looked at him like he was an ass. All he'd ever done was play up to the jerk. Jessica's natural assumption of him had pissed him off. Now all he wanted to do was prove to her that he could be something more, something different.

You want her pussy.

Pulling up beside her, he watched her remove her helmet flicking out her hair.

They walked into the diner together, taking a seat. Before he knew it they were being served breakfast. He'd never been served this fast unless Mia was the one doing all the work.

"You're not as big an asshole as Lydia made out," she said. "What makes me so special?"

"What do you mean? Can't I do anything good for you without my intentions being questioned?"

"Sure, you and I both know you fuck women and leave 'em. I'm not interested in joining that queue of women. Lydia told me you had a lot of women hating you but also a lot of women waiting for you at the clubhouse."

"Lydia talks too fucking much."

Jessica smiled. "Don't worry. I'm not going to tell."

He chuckled. "Why did you become a nurse?"

"I like to help people. I'm good at it."

"Is that the reason you're always on call?"

"I like my job, but let's not talk about work. I think we've gotten past that with you waiting for me. Let's enjoy breakfast and, erm, talk about something else."

"If you want." Snake was going to have this woman whether she knew it or not.

Chapter Eleven

Three days before Christmas

"Are you sure?" Devil asked. "Once you make this commitment there's no going back."

"I'm sure. I'm more than sure. Arrange the priest. I want to marry Brianna."

Lexie sat on one of the sofas in Devil's office, and she whistled.

"Are you sure?" Lexie asked. "Marriage is one hell of a commitment."

"I want her. There's no other woman for me. I'm in love with her. I've been fucking her without a condom. She's what I want." Death had thought about it seriously, and there was no other woman he wanted other than Brianna. He also believed she was in love with him as well. He was more than willing to take the risk.

"I'll talk to the priest. He'll marry you on Christmas Eve for the right fee." Devil flicked his pen on the notepad. "I take it you don't want anyone else to know what you're going to do?"

"You can tell the club. I'm not going to keep it a secret. After all the shit we've been through, I want her."

Devil sat back.

"Tell him, Devil."

"Tell me what?" Death looked behind him at Lexie then back at Devil.

"We saw the way you looked at her. Well, Lexie saw the way you looked at her, but Lexie also pointed out that you wouldn't do anything unless we pushed. I had every intention of forcing Brianna to make a decision about becoming a club whore, an old lady, or leaving. Lexie said you'd pick her as your woman."

Death shook his head. "I'm not worried. I want

her, and you're right. I needed a push to claim her."

"Good, I'll arrange this."

"One more thing," Death said.

"What?" Devil looked annoyed, and Death wondered what he'd interrupted when he knocked. Devil and Lexie were known for fucking anywhere.

The smirk on Lexie's face let him know he'd interrupted exactly that.

"Yeah, we're busy, Death. Tell me what shit you want to say then fuck off."

"I want to go after the man who bought Brianna."

"The one she refers to as Master?" Devil asked.

"I want him dead."

Silence descended on the room.

"She was sold by Ronald. Whoever took a woman and used her has got money, lots of it. You can also bet that money comes with a shitload of power." Devil leaned forward.

"I don't care."

"I do. We all barely came out of the Gonzalez business alive. We're no longer working with The Skulls. I'm not going to go hunting for a man I know nothing about. If he comes looking for her, the club will back you. Until then, enjoy your woman, enjoy the peace, and let's have Christmas without any bastard drama." Devil stood, moving around to perch on the edge of his desk. "I get your fears. I understand them. I feel it all the time I look at my woman. I'm not going to be hunting a man I don't know."

Death understood what Devil was saying. He would step back. If the man ever came out of the woodwork, he'd take the fight to him. No one was ever going to hurt Brianna again.

"Are we good?" Devil asked.

"We're good." Death shook his president's hand.

"Thank you."

"I'll call the priest. You make sure to have the bride."

He walked out of the office in time to hear Lexie giggling.

The priest wouldn't be called anytime soon. Death went in search of Brianna. He looked everywhere, and an hour later he was starting to lose him mind.

"Anyone seen Brianna?" he asked, going into the main room.

"She's in the men's toilet," June said, looking up from her cell phone.

"What the fuck's she doing in the toilet?" He went into the women's toilet to find it empty. Stepping inside the men's toilet he stopped. She wore rubber gloves and was on her hands and knees scrubbing the mess around the base of the toilet.

"Fucking disgusting," she said, muttering to herself.

Her red hair was bound up on top of her head.

"What are you doing?" he asked, folding his arms and leaning up against the sinks.

She jerked around to look at him. "I'm cleaning. Seriously, the smell coming from this room was toxic. Don't you men know how to keep clean?"

Shaking his head, he left his position by the sinks, grabbed Brianna around the waist, and hauled her up against his chest. He didn't wait for her to start fighting. Death carried her out of the room going upstairs to his own bathroom.

Putting her into the shower, he turned the water on, climbing in with her.

"What are you doing?" she asked.

He didn't speak as he removed the gloves and her clothes.

"Death?"

Leaning down he took one of her nipples into his mouth, cutting off all protest she would have made.

Her questions turned into long, loud moans.

When he was sure he had her where he wanted her, he started to wash her, making sure he caressed her at every turn.

Death carried her out of the shower, dumping her on the bed. He stared down at her body. The arousal was already taking him to the edge. He needed her, wanted her, and it wasn't dying down.

"I'm going to fuck you now, and you're going to let me." He gripped the length of his cock as she opened her thighs, revealing her creamy cunt. "No, on your knees." He knew what he wanted.

She went to her knees, presenting her curvy ass to him. He grabbed the condom from his drawer along with the lube. Death had spoken to her about what he'd do. For the last couple of days he'd been preparing her ass for his cock using his fingers.

He rolled the condom over his rock hard length before sliding a finger through her slit. She was soaking wet.

Applying a generous amount of lube to his cock, he made sure he was more than ready before preparing her ass for his invasion.

When they were both slick, he threw the tube away, gripped his length and slowly began to press against her ass. The tight ring of her muscles kept him out. He wasn't going to stop.

Slowly, he pushed into her ass, fucking her in small strokes until she started to fuck back against him. Within minutes he was all the way inside her, guiding her onto his length.

"Fucking perfect," he said.

"Fuck my ass," Brianna said.

He did exactly that, claiming her ass like he had her pussy and mouth. Brianna belonged to him, and within three days he'd have a ring on her finger to cement things. This love was not one sided, and with every second that passed, he knew it.

He plunged into her ass at the same time as he teased her clit. Only when she found her release did he allow himself the pleasure of finding his own. They came together, their moans echoing off the walls as they found bliss.

****

Christmas Eve

Brianna was going to tell him. She couldn't keep her feelings a secret anymore. The love she felt for Death was starting to hurt her as she didn't tell him. Several times over the last three days she'd tried to tell him the truth only to stop herself from saying anything.

She noticed several of the women were acting strangely as they looked toward her. The kids and even the men were having the time of their lives as they began to celebrate the festive season.

Frowning, Brianna wondered where Death had gone. That morning she'd woken up to find him gone. She'd not thought much of it when she didn't see him around the kitchen.

Lexie entered the kitchen, whistling.

"Have you seen Death?"

The other woman smiled. "He's waiting for you out there."

Brianna moved out of the kitchen going to the main room. She stopped at what she saw. Death stood talking with a priest while the club was sitting on either side. A makeshift altar had been created, and a carpet with rose petals had been made down the center.

"Death, what's going on?" she asked, looking up to him.

"Brianna." He spoke her name, moving down the aisle toward her. When he was in front of her, her heart hammered inside her chest as he went to his knee. "I'm completely, totally, in love with you. Will you do me the honor of becoming my wife?"

She opened her lips then stopped to close them. "You want to marry me?"

"I love you, baby."

Tears filled her eyes. "I love you, too." She stared at the ring he produced in his palm.

"I've been planning this for the last couple of days. I wanted to make this special for you, for us."

She went down to her knees, wrapping her arms around his neck. "I love you so much. I would be more than honored to become your wife."

He cupped her face, dropping a kiss to her lips.

"She said yes," Death said, yelling for them all to hear.

What happened next was so surreal to Brianna. She stood beside Death as they both faced the priest. There was no need for a white dress or all the other crap. This, to her, was perfect.

"I now pronounce you man and wife," the priest said.

Whistles, howls, and cheers of joy floated around her as she became Death's wife. She was his woman through and through.

Death didn't allow her to stick around. He picked her up in his arms and carried her up to their room.

Once they were over the threshold, Death made

his dirty demands of her. Brianna was more than happy to give him what he wanted.

She loved him, and this was the most perfect Christmas ever.

Epilogue

Watching Brianna and Death get married had struck Snake hard. He didn't understand what was going on inside him. The whole ceremony had been sweet, enjoyable, and yet all he could imagine was Jessica in his arms.

Their breakfast had been good, but since then he'd not spoken to her. He also hadn't fucked any of the other women at the club, much to June's disappointment. Snake knew June was getting a little too attached.

Leaving the clubhouse after Death carried his wife upstairs for some dirty sex, Snake snuck out. He climbed on his bike and made his way toward Jessica's house. When they'd finished breakfast he'd followed her to her house to find she lived in a small, modest house. Parking his bike outside of the house he found the door decorated in fairy lights. The season was in full swing, but something was missing.

He needed to do one thing, and then he could go back to the clubhouse without another thought on his mind.

Going up the steps, he knocked on Jessica's door, waiting for her to answer.

The lights were on letting him know she was home. The door opened to reveal Jessica on the other side.

"Snake, what are you doing here?" she asked.

"I loved having breakfast with you, but I didn't get the chance to do one thing."

"What?" she asked, frowning.

Stepping close to her, he reached out to cup her cheeks. She was warm while he was cold. This was what drew him to Jessica. She was the lightness he'd long given up on. Slamming his lips down on hers, he moaned at the taste of her.

He slid his tongue along her lip until she opened up to let him inside. The kiss deepened, and she gripped his arms. She didn't push him away but held onto him as he kissed her.

"Merry Christmas, Jessica," he said, turning away to leave.

"Merry Christmas, Snake."

The door closed, and he didn't look back. The kiss hadn't cured any of his problems. The kiss had only caused him more problems. He wanted her, and there was no way he was going to have her.

The End

www.samcrescent.com

DEATH'S DIRTY DEMANDS

BESTSELLING BBW ROMANCE
SPICY ROMANCE FOR REAL WOMEN

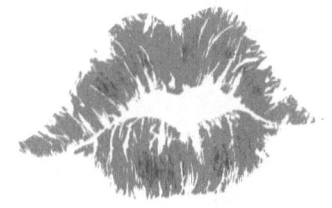

EVERNIGHT PUBLISHING ®

www.evernightpublishing.com